Gobstoppers, Shrimps and Sour Monkeys

FOSSEWAY WRITERS

2018 ANTHOLOGY:

a pick'n'mix of short stories and poems

FOSSEWAY WRITERS

ISBN: 9781980844563
Independently published, available as paperback or e-book.
2nd edition.

www.fossewaywriters.wordpress.com

Cover photograph and design by Nick Rowe
Compiled by Linda Cooper, Sean Gaughan and Nick Rowe
Edited and formatted by Nick Rowe

Contents

Dedication

This is for all those writers who have ever put pen to paper, or saved a file to electronic memory. It's also for all of those who want to do so and have the spirit to try.

Acknowledgements

There are many people who have contributed to Fosseway Writers over the past two decades, including members, speakers and occasional visitors. Several people have kept the show on the road by selflessly committing time and energy on obtaining speakers for workshops, managing the finances and promoting competitions. Every one of you has helped us to get here. Thank you! It's much appreciated!

The editor would like to thank those past members of the group who have kindly allowed the publication of some of the group's 'greatest hits' from the past couple of decades, namely Peter Day, Val Woolley, Joan Stephenson, Theresa Richmond, Kirsty Adlard and Peter Graves.

Fosseway Writers

We are a long-established group based in and around Newark, Nottinghamshire (itself situated on the old Roman 'Fosse Way', which is mostly now the route of the modern A46).

The aims of the group are to:
- provide a welcoming and stimulating environment for local writers;
- engage with, support and encourage local people who would like to try writing but don't know where to start;
- help members to improve and develop their writing skills;

...all through meetings, workshops, friendly socials and online interaction.

www.fossewaywriters.wordpress.com
fosseway.writers@mail.com
Find us on Facebook and Twitter via @FossewayWriters

THE END OF THE LINE

by Brenda Millhouse

WITH HER FRESHLY washed, almost waist length, golden blonde hair tied back she happily hummed to herself as she weighed, mixed and beat the mixture. The pale lemon sleeveless top and thin white cotton trousers emphasising the slimness of her body as she stretched across to empty the contents of the bowl into the already prepared tin. She couldn't help smiling contentedly as she gently closed the oven door. Then more broadly as she imagined his reaction to the finished product. The music relieving the boredom of the resultant washing up was interrupted by the telephone. She managed to reach it at the fourth ring, wiping her wet hands on the towel she had snatched up on her way from the kitchen before picking up the receiver. Within seconds the unseen smile at the sound of one of her favourite voices had vanished, and the blood drained from her face with it. Her shaking hands required two attempts to correctly replace the innocuous but now fearful instrument on its cradle. The conversation was already a blur, but the sheer panic was real, her thumping heart intent on pounding its way out of her body.

The bottle green radio remained blaring its now inappropriate jovial tune, and the doors were left unlocked as she tore from the small terraced house that had seemed so warm and secure just minutes ago. The car engine spluttered into life, and the old red Peugeot was frantically manoeuvred from its parking spot outside. She headed eastwards, towards Beacon Hill, the short wait at the traffic lights at its base seeming interminable. Then the drive up the steep incline of the hill itself, along the familiar road through Coddington, and the left turn into Stapleford Woods. The Rhododendrons in full multi-hued purple bloom meant it was early June, but she was ice cold. Why had it happened here? The memories of walking hand in hand with him along the flower lined glades fleetingly erased the horror of what she was heading towards, as she drove too fast for safety, past the beauty of what had been admired together on a romantic stroll just two days ago. It couldn't be true. She would have felt it.

An ambulance siren cut cruelly into her personal intimate silence, and the vehicle sped past. Her foot automatically pressed harder on the accelerator pedal, and she kept pace. She needed to be there too.

At last the right angle bend at the end of the woods and sight of the mature horse chestnut tree, which marked the junction of three roads. She'd admired it since her childhood, but its beautiful shapely branches only framed terror today. The bright green early summer foliage casting a late afternoon shadow over the mangled wreck in the ditch. The stylish Citroen with its distinctive pale silver paint work now possessed an unwanted extra; a freshly tinted deep red windscreen. The cause of the vivid splattered stain still slumped across the dashboard, but so very obviously beyond help. She was out of the car now, and it was then she screamed. The piercing sound of her anguish made the small group of paramedics and policemen gathered round the front of the car momentarily turn in her direction. Her strength as she struggled from the grip of a restraining arm was super human, and she reached the side of the car to look through the side window at a close up view of a nightmare. Trying desperately to avoid confrontation with unbearable hurt, she looked past it. She recognised the black briefcase lying amazingly unscathed on the passenger seat. The three brass initials glared back at her in the sunlight. Forcing her gaze to the driver's seat her eyes took in, and her brain somehow coped with, the sight of the contorted but limp broken body that occupied it. A voice inside shouted at her dulled senses, prodded the raw emotions, and she stared unbelievingly. Black hair, not mid brown beginning to go grey. The wide open but sightless eyes brown and not pale blue. The nightmare belonged to someone else.

The relief turned her legs to jelly, and the strong arm that had so recently tried to restrain her was now a comforting support as she slid to the ground against the still warm silver metal. After garbled explanations and a quick medical check by the insistent ambulance men, she was allowed to go. Not wanting to pass the torment or re-live their walk, she chose the route home through the smaller and less pretty part of the woods, along the narrow road that led to the busy A46. Turning left, she joined the steady stream of traffic heading back to Newark. Her overloaded mind was grateful for the congestion that made travelling at speed impossible. Totally unconscious of the passing scenery, her thoughts full of the destruction she had witnessed, she found herself driving along the more speedy short stretch of dual carriageway on the approach to the town. Nearly home now. What had happened to him? It was his car, his briefcase. But not his body. Please God not yet. WHERE WAS HE? She'd reached the double roundabout complex, had negotiated the first, and was waiting at the second. A lorry laden with over thirty tons of tubular metal girders took the adverse cambered bend just a few miles an hour too fast. The load strained at its chains, and the unstoppable strength of inertia snapped them like thin threads. The equally powerful force of gravity took over and the unleashed cargo rolled down on to the small red car below. She was dead in an instant.

Back in Wright Street the phone rang again. Ten rings before a breathless message was left on the answerphone. 'Hello darling, it's me. I'm sorry, but I'm going to be late home, someone's stolen my car, I'll try your mobile.'

In the small front room, now bathed in early evening sunlight, the mobile in its royal blue leather case trilled. Then like a baby bird abandoned by its mother, fell silent. The lovingly prepared contents of the oven had long since completed its cooking time, and the birthday cake slowly turned black.

ROSA'S CAFÉ

by Anne Howkins

BEN PUT HIS arms round me as I stood on the roof terrace, gazing out over the cityscape. I loved being up here, looking down on the narrow streets and higgledy rooftops. When the weather was good I would come up here to write, sure that the warmth of the sun worked its way to the words on the page. The sun was inching its way down through salmon pink clouds — it was going to be a spectacular sunset, just right for our party. The caterers were arranging the buffet, chatting quietly while someone was fussing over the wine — nothing but the best, served at the right temperature, would do for Ben.

'Penny for them,' he whispered.

'Oh, just thinking about Rosa's, how lucky we were.'

His body stiffened against mine as he stifled a barbed comment. He'd started to tire of any reference to the café. He'd been on edge for a few weeks now, and fobbed off any probing, no matter how tactful I tried to be. He just said things were hard at work, they had a difficult contract to get finished.

'Going to be a good night,' he said. 'Happy birthday to us.' By some quirk of fate we shared a birthday, two years apart.

He kissed my shoulder, and as I turned to face him his phone buzzed. He looked at the screen and walked away.

'That's Jim just parking up, he's cutting it a bit fine.' Jim always volunteered to DJ at our parties, and was running out of time to get his decks set up. As Ben disappeared to let him in, I hoped his affection was a sign that whatever was worrying him was sorted out. And I let my thoughts drift back to Rosa.

I met Jim and Ben in a café fifteen years ago; a scruffy little place with a grimy door window obscured by faded flyers for time-past yoga classes, reiki practitioners and crystal readings. The sort of café that usually delivered organic tisanes and wholemeal rock cakes. It was on a street that had seen better days, with boarded up shops and student lets, next door to a dental surgery. But it was my place. I used to bury myself at the corner table, the one overshadowed by the Dali print with the dripping clock. The magazine rack next to the table overflowed with dog-eared publications , all at least a decade out of date. It was the only place you could get Russian caravan tea without a 'never heard of that!' Mismatched, chipped crockery that probably wasn't the most hygienic, and it was better not to look too closely at Rosa's hands as she dished up plates of bean stew at lunchtime. I could make a pot of tea last a whole morning, and Rosa knew when to leave well alone. And when to offer an ear and a shoulder if needed. Nobody knew when Rosa opened her café, where she'd come from, really who she was.

Somehow I'd walked unseeing past that door every morning, on my way from dingy bed-sit to self-imposed stint at the library, head brimming with ideas that melted away the moment I opened a notebook. I spent a few hours pretending to write before my evening shift at the call centre. Every day I would tell myself it would be worth it when I finally got that dream job on a national paper. When you start your degree, all bright and shiny, brimming with expectation and ambition, you don't really consider the statistics, the tales of drudgery and failure. How could you? So every day I trudged down the street, each step taking me further towards self-pity and humiliation. I would sit amongst the old men bickering over who got the Times first. Apparently the early bird caught the crossword.

I was on the verge of giving it all up that dank, wet winter morning. Head down, I grimly trod my way through the rain that seeped downwards through my old raincoat and upwards through the worn out pair of boots that desperately needed re-soling. I tripped over a hobbledy paving stone and launched myself onto the pavement, going over on my ankle as I lost my balance. I lay there, the effort of getting up past me. I couldn't stop the tears. I was wringing wet and cold, and I could already feel my ankle swelling inside my sodden boot.

A hand touched my shoulder. A voice with an indeterminable, possibly eastern European, accent asked gruffly if I was OK. A small rotund form helped me to my feet and checked that I could stand without support. She picked up my scattered pens and notebooks. I couldn't see properly through the film of rain and tears veiling my face, but somehow there was a halo of light above me. Slowly I realised that there was a gaudy fairground sign above my head. A red and yellow curved arrow, bare light bulbs around its perimeter, pointing through the murk to a dimly lit doorway.

My rescuer ushered me from cold wet into a warm fug and steered me to the corner table that would become my home. She peeled off my drenched coat, gently unzipped boots, lifted the sore ankle onto a chair, covered it in a bag of peas wrapped in a red gingham tea towel, and put a glass beaker of steaming amber liquid in front of me. .

'I am Rosa,' she said. 'This is my place, I take care of you. You are my friend.'

As simply as that, she really did take care of me.

The place was empty for a while, just me and Rosa. Then, as the skewed clock above Rosa's counter ticked away, others joined us. Nobody placed an order. Rosa just put drinks and food in front of her customers. Some people opened laptops and bent heads seriously over their screens. Others scribbled in notebooks, a few chatted. Nobody paid me any real attention other than a slight tip of the head, a shy smile, a quick hi. But I didn't feel like a stranger.

Each morning I would head for that amber glow and join her crowd of ragamuffin hopeless cases. It seemed that we all wanted something, but none of us knew how to get it. How to climb out of the ruts we'd so carefully carved for ourselves. The group would be static for a while, then a familiar face would no longer appear. After a little while, someone new would arrive to take their place. Rosa never made introductions, she didn't really talk to us, but when she did you knew to listen. Most of the time she just stood behind her counter, hair wrapped in the faded burgundy turban that smelt of bergamot and petitgrain, arms folded across a stout no-nonsense body. She just watched and listened, dispensed food and drinks, and rarely proffered a few words of advice...

And that's how she steered me from misery to hope.

'Talk to Jim, he help you.'

'Ben — you take Claudia to cinema.'

'Claudia, you see this ad?'

Ben started coming to sit at my table. We'd sit opposite each other, me writing, him doing something on his laptop. Somehow I found our silent companionship a catalyst for ideas and felt myself grow more confident. I started to take a snatch of conversation I'd overheard or something interesting I'd seen and turn it into a piece I might actually be able to send to the local rag.

Jim knew someone, who knew someone else, whose sister worked on the Herald. He got me her phone number and she agreed to put a couple of my articles in front of the editor.

Turned out that Jim was dyslexic, so I helped him write job application letters.

And that's how Rosa's worked. We were a little community, helping and encouraging each other. We never questioned the lack of new customers. There was no passing trade, just the regular group. Rosa's private club, we joked.

Ben got his break first. He'd been invited to join an IT start up. Not much money to start, but it was a foot on the ladder. Starting in a couple of weeks. I was his lucky charm he said. That was the day he kissed me for the first time.

Then the editor of the Herald asked to see me. Someone was retiring, everyone else was taking a step up the ladder and the bottom rung was mine if I wanted it. That night I stayed at Ben's flat.

We were bursting to tell Rosa our news. When we turned the corner into that familiar street there was something missing. No fairground sign pointing to Rosa's. Must be broken we said. We tried the door handle, nothing happened. There was no light from inside. We scrubbed at the glass with our elbows, trying desperately to peer inside. Ben knocked on the door, expecting Rosa to rush up with some excuse for the door being locked. Then he hammered at the wooden frame with his fist, shouting Rosa's name.

'What's going on?'

The adjacent door opened, revealing a balding man wearing a pristine white tunic and black trousers.

'What do you want?'

'The café,' Ben started 'we've come to Rosa's'

'Not that again,' the dentist looked resigned 'I've been here for twenty years and that café's not been open in all that time. Every so often someone turns up and asks about this Rosa. You must have got the wrong street.' He slammed his door shut.

'No he's wrong,' I said 'he must be, we were here yesterday.'

Ben pointed upwards. The sign was dirty, bits of plastic fluttered in the bulb holders, which were all empty.

'That sign's not been working for ages.'

'How can that be...?' I just couldn't understand it, how could Rosa just disappear? The dentist must have been lying, maybe he resented her in some way. We stood there for ages, amazed and uncomprehending. I started crying, then Ben wrapped his arms around me. He told me we didn't need Rosa, we had each other. No, we couldn't explain what had happened, we just had to accept it. He was right, our life as a couple started that day. We were so right together, how we'd met didn't matter.

My confidence grew and I was offered a column on a bigger paper. Ben taught me how to set up a blog and that led to other work. Finally that glittering career in journalism seemed within my grasp. His IT company hit the IT wave at just the right time, work just appeared from nowhere. We bought a flat in on old mill building, and spent a fortune furnishing it. Life just couldn't get any better we kept telling ourselves. Every so often we'd raise a glass of wine to Rosa, wherever she was. And sometimes we'd walk along that street, hoping that the sign might be lit up, or that the door would open. Each time we went, the place looked more and more desolate.

'Hi Claudia!' A gaggle of girlfriends woke me from the daydream. Ben appeared, schmoozing as only he could, revelling in the attention.

It was a good party, even a great one, until about midnight. I'd hardly seen Ben all night, we were both busy catching up with people, listening to old jokes and new stories. The food had been amazing everyone said, and trust Ben to find that incredible white wine, where did he get the time? Then Jim started playing some smoochy songs. I wanted it to be just Ben and me, dancing on our rooftop. I looked round, asked a few people if they'd seen him. Shrugged shoulders were my answer.

I went down into the kitchen. I had to shout to make myself heard. Everyone thought he was outside. Something made me go downstairs again to the bedrooms. I heard Ben's voice from our room, and opened the door..

'Come and dance ...' my voice trailed into nothing. Ben was one side of the bed, buttoning his shirt. An auburn haired young girl was just pulling her T shirt over her head.

'Claudia don't...' Ben's voice trailed behind me as I ran out, down the stairs and out onto the street. I kept running, turning corners, through back alleys, just running away from Ben. I was heading for Rosa's.

When I got there I was gasping, trying to suck air into empty lungs. My legs wobbled and I crumpled to the pavement. The pain in my chest was unbearable, I curled into the tightest ball I could make.

And then that touch. That voice. I looked up to see the familiar fairground sign, blazing above us for all to see.

'Come inside dear, Rosa will help.'

THE TRUNK

by Barbara Hatton

No! After forty years, she couldn't mean it. Once again Clive read the letter that his wife had left propped up on the hall table. Left him! And he about to retire. What about the plans he had made to do things together? He was going to treat himself to a new car so that they could make trips to local beauty spots; join the bowls club; take up fishing; things that they could both do. He had even thought he might get Claire a new bike for her shopping and visits to the library. But she had left him.

His anger was rising. The white lilac tree was there at the end of the lawn. Claire had planted it when they first moved into Willow Close. Clive didn't approve. He considered lilac a frivolous tree. A nice conifer or a good hornbeam would have been much more suitable. That was one of Claire's failings — too concerned with outward appearances. His mother had warned him.

During their early years even the food she prepared was inappropriate — curries and Italian dishes, stuff like that. Clive had to put a stop to it. He had managed to curb her flights of fancy, demanding plain food, like his mother cooked. His wife was always wanting him to redecorate and refurnish. Only three weeks ago she had suggested that when he retired he could repaint the hall. Why? He did it ten years ago.

So many thoughts flitted through his mind. Claire wanting to go to Spain or France for a holiday when she knew perfectly well that they always went to Scarborough. Asking for trips to the theatre when they had a very good telly. She even tried to persuade him to let her accompany him to The Bull when he made his Friday night foray for a pint with Joe. Totally unsuitable for a woman. He always brought her a bag of chips in. He wasn't selfish.

The sight of the blossom-laden lilac fuelled his anger. 'Right' he muttered. 'That tree comes down tomorrow. Teach her a lesson. When she comes crawling back —as she will — her precious lilac will be gone.'

He made himself a meal and then settled in his chair to think. It would be as well to get a good solicitor, for there was a remote chance that she might not return. The bank must be notified. Cut off her source of income. So many issues to be sorted out but the destruction of the tree was top priority.

He was up early the next morning. It was a crisp, fair day as he attacked the tree with the cross-saw. By lunch-time the limbs of the lilac littered the lawn. Clive made a brief break for coffee and a sandwich. He felt a little weary, being unused to such energetic work. Claire did the garden, mowing the lawn regularly. He was too tired after working all day and he liked to keep his week-ends free.

He went out again to make the final assault. Only the trunk remained to be demolished. No need for the ladder now. An axe would be quicker than the saw, he thought. He began to wield the tool, swiping at the ruined tree. At the fourth stroke he felt a searing pain shoot up his arm and across his chest. Dizzily he staggered sideways and collapsed. With a screeching creak the trunk toppled and crashed down on Clive's head, crushing his skull.

At the inquest the pathologist reported that it wasn't the heart attack that killed Mr Grudgin but the tree trunk.

Sitting in the court Claire sighed when the verdict of misadventure was announced. She felt some sympathy for Clive but her real sadness was for the loss of her lovely lilac. 'Oh well,' she thought 'I'll plant another one when I move back in.'

Now, of course, Willow Close was hers, as was Clive's pension and his substantial bank account.

ALL TUCKED UP, NICE AND COSY

by Jackie Leitch

Have you ever noticed that there seems to be a malign force at work in the universe? One that delights in ruining your best laid plans? Annoying isn't it? It's happened to me before. I'll bet it has to you, too. You know how it goes - after weeks of rain, at last it turns warm and sunny. You decide on a barbecue. The table's laid, friends invited, beer cooling, and the barbeque glowing nicely. Then the heavens open.

Or, you organise a weekend away at the seaside with the boyfriend. TripAdvisor recommended hotel booked, tick; car filled with petrol, tick; restaurant table reserved, tick; even a luxury picnic in the boot for the journey down. The phone goes and it's him saying his Dad's had an accident at work and is in intensive care. Your response is perfectly reasonable.

'Well, you can't do anything, can you? Can't we go anyway?' you ask, 'After all, it's all booked, be a shame to cancel', and he gets angry and unpleasant about it and you end up rowing and breaking up.

You too? No? Ok, maybe it's just me, then. Anyway, this was turning into one of those situations. Malign force at work with a vengeance.

The body at my feet twitches once, and then is still. I stand looking down at it and –

'Damn it.' I can't help it, the words just burst from me. Complications I don't need, and this death is not part of the plan. I know, just know, there'll be hell to pay over this if I can't find a way to retrieve the situation.

I nudge the body hopefully with the toe of my boot. Maybe I'm wrong, perhaps blood will once again pump through the arteries and the corpse will spring to life like Frankenstein's monster – a corpse no more. Of course, I know better than that, I've seen enough dead bodies to know one when I see one, and this one was as dead as any I'd seen before.

Pursing my lips in thought, I muse, 'What to do, what to do?' irritated by this distraction.

The evening had started well. I had my instructions clear. Find the host – one Jonathon Charles Vale, developer and builder extraordinaire. Possessor of a fortune but, sadly for him, no wife. However, he had a considerable appetite for the good life, including 'not so good' women. This was my way in as I could claim, with some justification, to being a 'not so good' woman, and my employer was keen that I explore that side of my personality on his behalf and retrieve some – shall we say, awkward paperwork and photos? These had come into Mr Vale's possession via his contacts with organised crime. My employer dearly wished to have them back. Hence my attendance at this lovely soiree. It was all planned to a tee. Find and lure Jonathon Charles into the appropriate room, slip something into his drink, keep him occupied until said 'something' takes effect, relieve him of the safe key, retrieve the items, hand them to my employer, receive my cut and fade into the distance. That had been the plan. Certainly, Jonathon Charles was pliant and interested. I was wearing a low-cut, split to the thigh dress from

Donna Versace, of course he was pliant and interested. I wasn't even sure that I needed any chemical assistance, but true to the plan, I dropped just a tiny drop or two into his drink. Once in the room he proved to be extremely compliant - and then! Dramatic change of plan required. I had and still have, a body on the carpet, rather than a happy bunny who will hand over the necessary key without any fuss. Pity really, he was rather nice looking in a public-school sort of way. Oh well, easy come, easy go. On the way in, I noticed a rather tasty waiter who would certainly provide more fun than a drugged and – as it now turns out – dead, builder, however extraordinaire.

Dragging my thoughts back to the matter in hand I wonder what to do with this damned corpse. Someone is bound to come looking sooner or later and if I leave it here it'll be found and they'll raise the alarm, and that definitely is not in the plan. I look around me. There's got to be somewhere I can dump it.

Oh, for crying out loud, now my phone's vibrating. It's just one damned interruption after another! Why can't people leave me alone to get on with it?

'What?' I snap in a harsh whisper.

'Just wondered how it's going?'

I pause. Best to be upfront, I decide.

'Okay. Umm - a slight hiccup, nothing to worry about.'

There's a strained silence. 'Hiccup?'

'Mmmm, a small hitch, I can handle it.'

There's a sort of hissing sound at the other end of the phone. I give it a shake before realising that it's my caller.

'Look, it's vital that this goes off exactly to plan, Nell. I'm counting on you. You said it'd be easy. No problem, you said.'

'And it isn't a problem.' I raise my voice, then realise what I'm doing and throttle back to a whisper. 'Yes, I know. Don't go on. I'm handling it. I said, didn't I? Just let me get on.' I go to end the call and then think of something else. 'And don't ring again.'

While I'm talking on the phone I'm looking hard for hiding places for this nuisance of a body. Honestly, he can't have been in very good health, despite his sturdy appearance. How was I to know he'd keel over like that? He had barely a sip and bam, over he went. Heart at a guess. Well, what's done is done. I give myself a quick motivational talk. You know what they say, no plan ever survives first implementation. It's how you deal with a setback that counts. Time to get dealing. Meanwhile, he's still there, going cold and I need to get rid before he stiffens up and I can't move him. The best I can do is to hide him in plain sight. So, I drag him to the big sofa on the back wall, haul him into a prone position, and with a cushion tucked under his head and the fluffy throw from the back of the sofa tucked round him like a blanket, I'm done. He looks comfortable, as if he's in a deep, sexually-satiated, alcohol-induced sleep. I'm happy with that.

Voices approach and I snarl in irritation. Another bloody interruption. At this rate the party will be over and I will still be in here trying to finish this ill-fated job. I duck down behind the wing chair. The door opens and a bright slice of light illuminates the dim room.

'Ah, there he is,' slurs a male voice. 'Sleeping it off, eh?' A woman giggles and says something I don't hear. 'No' the man replies, 'Not in there with him asleep, that would be too weird.' The door closes and I hear them stagger off to find an unoccupied room.

Right, so now all I have to do is find the paperwork and photos I've been contracted to steal, and job done. Apart from getting out undetected. It's been an interesting few hours, what with the unexpected body, but I think it's gone pretty well, all things considered. The key from the corpse's pocket opens the desk drawer and there is the key for the old-fashioned safe behind the Reubens copy over the fireplace. Paperwork and photos safely stashed in my Fendi handbag, I slip out back to the party and stay just long enough for another glass of champagne and a brief flirtation with the handsome waiter, before gathering up my fur coat and leaving in the Range Rover. Sadly, the bag, coat and car have to go back tomorrow but for the rest of tonight I intend to enjoy some luxury. The hotel room is booked and paid for – on expenses, of course.

I pat the thigh of the gorgeous young waiter sitting beside me, 'Nearly there, darling,' I say. 'And the night is still young.'

A-Z OF WAR

by Diane McClymont

Aeroplanes Bomb Cities.
Destruction!
Explosions, Flames, Gunfire.
Helpless Innocents Jailed, Killed.
Loved-ones Murdered.
Nervous, Oppressed People Question.
Rebel Soldiers Terrorise.
Useless, Violent War!
Xenophobia Yields Zero.

PERFECT

By Linda Cooper

'NOT TODAY FRANK, please. It's too hot.'

Frank glares at me, his perfectly shaped brown eyes penetrating my thoughts, sending a shiver of fear down my spine.

'You know what I told you Colleen; you'll wear the gloves until the day before my parent's anniversary party. Go on; get to the shops before all the best stuff's been picked over.'

'But Frank, I look ridiculous wearing gloves in this weather. Everyone stares at me as if I'm crazy.'

'Remember when everyone stared because you were so amazingly flawless? That's the woman I married and that's the woman I want back. No more arguments and pick my suit up from the cleaners on the way back.'

There's no point continuing the debate. I'm tempted to tear off the stupid gloves and deposit them in the nearest waste bin but know what would happen if I did. It sounds ridiculous I know; a grown woman being dictated to in this day and age, but not everyone has a husband like Frank.

My thoughts drift into the past as I make my way to the small shopping centre in town, doubled under a heavy load of self pity. Head down, eyes focussed on the paving stones but still painfully aware of the questioning glances of passers-by. What sort of girl wears gloves in the middle of summer? Ask *him,* I want to scream.

Frank and I enjoyed a whirlwind romance at university and I foolishly wanted a wedding ring on my finger before anyone else succeeded in snapping him up. I remember the best man at our wedding describing us as the 'perfect couple.' Within weeks I realised Frank's idea of perfection was to dominate our lives and that he'd go to twisted, bizarre extremes to satisfy his ambitions. It was not, as I'd imagined a marriage made in heaven, more in error.

Just a few weeks after the wedding I discovered my husband was not the unblemished man I'd believed him to be. We, or rather he, purchased a compact new house on a private estate. Frank insisted he'd earn enough to keep us both so I'd not sought employment. I thought it rather sweet and old-fashioned of Frank; wanting me to stay at home and was quite prepared to channel my energies into creating domestic bliss. One afternoon, satisfied all chores were completed for the day I sat watching an old weepy on the television when Frank burst through the door like a shell from a cannon.

'There's some dust on the hall table,' he bawled almost hysterically, his perfect, full lips trembling as if he'd discovered a corpse. I tried to laugh it off but after a while I realised our home must be as spotless and sterile as an operating theatre to avoid Frank's wrath.

Then the day I burnt the evening meal; it was only a sharp clip on the cheek, but enough to convince me Frank has a real problem. He punished my incompetence by arranging for his mother to stay with us until I'd learnt to cook real family meals.

I've never had time for my mother-in-law and partly blame her for Frank's behaviour; raising him to believe he's the perfect male specimen and nothing is good enough for him, especially me.

My cooking improved as the relationship deteriorated, but providing the house was cleaned daily from top to bottom and there were no culinary disasters, life was tolerable. After the birth of our second child however, Frank's obsessive criticism turned personal.

'You're out of shape, Colleen. You've put too much weight on and your figure's getting flabby. It won't do, you know.' Tears stung my eyes, but I wasn't brave enough to argue that it wasn't his perfect body that had endured the trials of pregnancy and childbirth.

Under Frank's supervision I was forced to take up rigorous exercise routines; producing top quality meals for the family whilst existing on rabbit food myself. Both my weight and self-esteem plummeted, but that was not to be the end of it. For my next birthday, Frank presented me with an appointment for cosmetic surgery, silicone implants. He may as well have written 'Your tits are too small,' on the accompanying birthday card. There was no pleasing this man it seemed.

I know, I should have left him but you tell me where an unemployed mother of two young children turns? And I suppose, deep down, I hoped Frank would soon be satisfied and all this would stop.

Physically, I was nearing the perfect image Frank desired, but mentally and emotionally I was falling apart. Had cigarettes or alcohol been allowed in our home I suspect I'd have turned to them to calm my frayed nerves. Instead, without even realising, I began to bite my fingernails. Only lightly and occasionally at first, but soon seizing every opportunity to sink my teeth into what was left of my nails and the flesh surrounding them. Of course, it wasn't long before Frank noticed, almost causing a cardiac arrest. Hence the gloves; I've had to wear them now, day and night throughout the longest, hottest summer on record. It's been so uncomfortable and embarrassing.

All the time I'm loading the groceries into my basket I can feel the eyes of the check out girl and other customers on my covered hands and I can't escape the shop fast enough. Similar reactions at the dry cleaners where I hastily pick up Frank's suit; it didn't need cleaning, it was immaculate when I brought it in, though not in the eyes of Mr Impeccable. How I wish something or someone would damage his perfect image for once.

Two weeks later we sit around his parent's perfect mahogany dining table, surrounded by immaculate crockery and food. The discussions rarely include me; I'm just here as a decoration, complete with impeccably manicured and painted nails. Frank seems happy, his mother gloating over his faultless appearance and ignoring eye contact with me. I'm bored and frustrated; anger and resentment bubbling like molten lava underneath my calm, polished exterior.

Later that night, Frank rolls his perfectly toned, tanned body onto mine. There's a moment's hesitation before he announces, 'Aren't you glad I made you beautiful again? Maybe you could do with a tummy tuck though.'

My scarlet talons find his face in the dark. He will carry the scars from the scratches on his cheeks for the rest of his life and I will carry on *my* life without him. Perfect.

THE PARTY

By N.K. Rowe

MARIA OPENED THE door with a smile. 'Hello! So good of you to come over, come on in!' She stepped aside, allowing Richard and Hanna to enter the hallway. 'Go through, please,' she added and then peered outside before closing the door.

She followed them through into the lounge. 'I'm afraid Peter has probably been held up at work again, but he shouldn't be too long. May I take your coats?' she asked.

'Oh, that man of yours is always working hard,' said Hanna as she slipped off her new pale blue coat and handed it to Maria. 'Not like this one, always looking for the easy win.' She glared playfully at Richard.

He beamed a Hollywood smile back at her and held up a bottle. 'Yes, it's true, but at the moment I seem to have the winning touch!' He handed the bottle and his coat to Maria. 'Happy birthday, Maria. I assume you like a good Châteauneuf-du-Pape?'

'Oh, Richard, you shouldn't have!' she said, blushing and trying to keep the coats from sliding from her arms. 'I hope you haven't spent a lot of money on it.'

'Not at all,' he replied with a roguish grin, 'I know a guy who knows a guy...'

'Richard's always on the lookout for another contact to further his wheeler-dealing,' said Hanna apologetically, 'but sometimes I have to agree that they do come in useful.'

'I'll just go and put these away,' said the laden hostess and she disappeared through a second doorway. 'Can I get you a drink before we eat?' she asked from the kitchen.

Hanna raised her eyebrows in silent warning to Richard. He shrugged innocently with upturned hands.

Maria re-appeared with a couple of bottles. 'I'm afraid we don't have much to choose from,' she said studying the labels one after another. 'There's bourbon or cognac. And I think we have some Pernod and schnapps somewhere too. Or you could have a soda?'

Richard took the bourbon from her and examined the label. 'Hmm, Kentucky; sounds good. I'll try a shot of this, thanks Maria.' He was aware of Hanna's eyes on him and he added, 'Just a small one though, eh? I feel guilty about drinking Peter's best booze without him here to enjoy it as well.'

Maria turned to Hanna who responded with a tight smile. 'The cognac sounds great, Maria. Just a small one for me too.'

Maria busied herself with producing glasses and pouring out the drinks, the soft chink of glass and flow of alcohol mixing with the sound of the radio talking to itself in the background. Richard looked out of the window at the sun setting on the street, touching everything out of the shadows with rays of gold and copper. Hanna stepped over to the fireplace and looked at the birthday cards arranged on the mantelpiece. 'May I?' she asked, pointing to the cards.

Maria looked up, holding two glasses of spirits. 'Of course, go ahead.' She came over to them and handed them their drinks. Hanna took hers in her right hand and lifted a card with her left, using her thumb to deftly flick it open to reveal the message and names within. It was apparently from the Rosenbergs next door.

'I've had one from David, my brother, who's studying in England,' said Maria and she nodded at the next card in line. 'That one's from Michael and Ursula in Pennsylvania. He's doing really well with a company there, but I forget exactly what it is he does. It's hard to keep track these days.'

'It certainly is,' agreed Richard. 'Technology keeps advancing, old companies go bust, new innovators come along. You have to be sharp to make sure you're not siding with yesterday's world, otherwise you'll be unemployed before you know it.'

'Not that Peter's in that situation, of course,' said Hanna, glaring at Richard.

'Good God, no,' said Richard quickly, 'Peter's in telecommunications. Cutting edge stuff. He'll be fine.' He made a face back at Hanna.

Maria forced a smile. 'I'll just get myself a drink,' she said and turned back to the bottles at the other end of the room.

The man on the radio filled the awkward silence.

'He sounds angry,' said Hanna, trying to lighten the mood.

'Oh, it's that goddamned politician guy again,' said Richard. 'What's his name? The one with the ridiculous hair that he keeps pushing across his head.'

The sound of a key opening the front door came from the hallway and a man's voice called out, 'Hi honey, sorry about the time. Are Richard and Hanna...?' The sentence stopped as Peter's head poked into the room. 'Ah, yes you are. Sorry I'm late. Let me just put my things away.'

'No problem,' Richard called after him as he stepped away from the lounge door, 'we've only been here a few minutes.'

Peter re-entered in shirtsleeves and pointed to Richard's drink. 'Still long enough for you to make a start on my best bourbon, though,' he said cheerily.

'And I've got one ready for you too, darling,' said Maria, handing over a glass of amber whiskey.

'Thanks honey,' he said, taking the drink, 'and I guess we should raise our glasses and toast to Maria: happy birthday!'

'Happy birthday!' echoed their guests.

As they paused to sip their drinks, the angry man on the radio caught Peter's attention. 'Oh for God's sake, why have we got him on?'

'I don't know,' said Maria, 'I'd only just turned it on when Richard and Hanna arrived. I hadn't had chance to find a music station.'

'He's an odious little shit,' said Peter, 'saying he wants to make the country great again, giving people something different than the usual career politicians, but he's just a noisy empty vessel.' He strode over to the radio and turned it off. 'All he's interested in is his own ego and finding scapegoats. And there's an ugly, violent side to some of his supporters. I can't think of a single good thing to say about him.'

'Umm, well,' said Richard, cagily, 'at least he isn't a communist.'

'Who is he, anyway?' asked Hanna. 'I don't pay any attention to politics. And quite rightly so, by the sound of things.'

'His name,' said Peter with a grimace, 'is Adolf Hitler and if he ever becomes Chancellor... we're emigrating.'

WAYS OF SEEING

by Peter Day

Marilyn:
varied combinations
of ten different colours;
this series of lurid images
challenges us.
Seeing her as a product,
a packaged consumer item,
a subject of envy
constituting glamour,
he aimed to de-mystify her.
But the dream of glamour
is personal to the dreamer;
as Marilyn said
you may envy me,
but I'm not always the person
I appear to be.

CROSSING ROADS

By Sean Gaughan

I WAS MAKING MY way along Trumpington Street, heading for Cambridge Market, my mind completely unsettled. Although a huge problem that had been troubling me for almost a year had been resolved for me the previous day, and I now knew what my course must be for the foreseeable future, I was far from elated. One burden had been lifted off my mind, only to be replaced by another - the oppressive weight of emptiness.

My mood was as changeable as the late February weather; the sky, now lowering, now briefly lifting, matched my own feelings. Whilst I no longer had painful choices to make, indeed none were open to me, and in all probability my guilt would now remain undiscovered, my appreciation of these facts was tempered by a cutting sense of loneliness and rejection; the painful knowledge that something that had been exciting and pleasurable was gone forever.

My gaze downcast, I noted only the remaining winter leaves clogging the drains, clinging wetly to the exposed roots of the lime trees set at intervals in the pavement. I could see only the miserable relics of last year, never lifting my head to notice the earliest Spring buds just beginning to show on the branches of the trees. My thoughts isolated me from the ever-present swirling mass of humanity that always permeates every street and alleyway of an ancient university city.

I was startled out of my misery by a strong, genial female voice that I recognised immediately, even before I discerned its source within the crowd. It was that of a former work colleague whom I had not seen for about eighteen months, apart from, that is, a very brief meeting around six months ago on a railway platform where we were both about to board trains going in opposite directions.

'Hi Tom, how are you doing?' she called gaily from twenty yards away as she slanted across the road to my side, skilfully dodging the traffic. 'Lovely to see you,' she said, with a warm smile and laughter in her voice. We hugged and stood back a pace to appraise each other. Victoria and I had got on supremely well when we worked together in the laboratory. We magnified each other's strengths and mitigated our weaknesses which, I say confidently and truthfully, were very few. We developed a perfect synergy which enabled us to accomplish a great deal. Consummate professionals, we strived towards perfection and revelled in the outcomes we achieved.

There was never a sexual relationship between us; in fact we didn't socialise outside of work, although within the lab we were very close, totally at ease with each other. Victoria knew that I was married although she had never met Sarah. I somehow knew that she had been married and that there had been an amicable parting of the ways long before she joined the firm. She seemed happy to live on her own and was never lacking friends.

Not having seen each other for a long while there were of course some general enquiries to be made - the 'what have you been doing with yourself?' sort of thing. I said to her 'You look really well, really happy.'

'I am,' she said. 'I'm in a relationship now. He's taking me on holiday to America next month.'

'That sounds great,' I said, 'very promising. I'm pleased for you. Have you moved in together or shouldn't I ask?'

'No. His divorce is dragging on a bit. But we will soon. At present he's sharing a slummy bed-sit on Drummer Street with a pal of his. I haven't seen it of course. The living quarters of two males in a small space is something I don't need to observe at close quarters.' She pulled a face as she said this, feigning abhorrence at the thought and I laughed. I didn't think to ask her why he hadn't moved in with her instead. I knew she had a decent place of her own. 'But enough about me, Tom. I'm concerned about you. I *have* to say this: you do not appear well.'

'Oh.'

'I mean it, Tom; sorry to be so blunt about it though.'

'I'm okay. I've just had a bout of gastroenteritis and I had the 'flu for a month before that. But I'm much better now.'

'Come on, Tom. It's more than that. The last time I saw you - at the station when we didn't have time to talk - you looked ghastly. You were haggard. I could see that you'd lost a lot of weight. I thought perhaps that you'd got some awful disease. I couldn't get that brief meeting out of my mind for a long time. You still look thin and drawn and - oh, I can't describe it - distant, somehow. Spaced out, you know? What *is* the matter with you?'

I looked at my feet guiltily. I realised that I desperately needed to talk and Victoria was the perfect listener. She was unshockable, non-judgemental, never one to criticise others. 'How much time have you got, Vicky?' I asked.

'I've got all day. I was only on my way to squander some money in the sales.'

'Look,' I said, 'there's a café over the road. It's not bad, I go in there sometimes. I could do with a coffee and a chat right now.'

We crossed back over and entered. I paid for two coffees at the counter and carried them across to a table near a corner. The café was half empty but I felt that I needed as much seclusion as possible. Victoria took a seat with her back to the wall; I faced her, elbows on the table, fingers interlaced in the attitude of a supplicant, although why I felt so guilty I don't know. Victoria wouldn't judge me.

'So Tom, what's bothering you? You're *not* well, are you?'

'No, I'm not. But not in the way you're thinking.' I scraped my hand over my head and down on to the back of my neck; I could feel my pulse racing at the thought of finally letting go. I took a deep breath and continued. 'I've been having an affair for the past year. I guess the burden of guilt has been weighing me down.'

If Victoria had been surprised she didn't show it. 'Does Sarah know?'

'No, she doesn't.' I stared down at my coffee. 'And she won't now. It's ended. But I still feel bad about it. Largely for selfish reasons. I wanted it to go on, despite the guilt.' I raised my eyes again and managed a weak smile. 'I feel very mixed up.'

She nodded slightly and gave a small smile in return as she lifted her cup. 'How serious was it?'

'Well, it started as a bit of joking about, you know. Good humoured banter but nothing physical. And then we found ourselves at a party where... where we just clicked. It was *electric*, passionate in a way that...' I stumbled over words that had been kept locked away for so long. 'And it was meaningful, not just 'a bit of fun'. At least, to me anyway.' I toyed with my cup. Victoria let me continue at my own pace. 'But I kept on thinking about Sarah, about the deception. What would it do to her if she found out?'

Victoria remained impassive. 'You could have just left her. You don't have any kids to worry about. She would have been hurt, of course. And angry. But you could both have started out again. You're not so old and there's plenty of fish in the sea, as they say. She would have got over it.'

I shook my head gently and felt the anxiety rise again. 'No, Vicky. She wouldn't.'

'Why not? How can you be so sure? People have to come to terms with things they don't like. It happens all the time.'

'Sarah, well, she's not like that. You've never met her so you wouldn't know.'

'Know what?'

'She's very highly strung. She's not good at coping. She calls me her rock. If I left she'd be a complete psychological wreck. She couldn't manage on her own.'

'Tom, you can get help with those sorts of problems. Counselling and stuff. People can get better. Perhaps she needs the space to be herself.'

'She's had help; lots of it. It's done no good. When she was sixteen she was waiting to cross a road with her little sister. There was an accident of some kind and a car mounted the pavement. It missed Sarah by inches but it killed her sister. Sarah has always blamed herself, she believes she should have taken more care of her sister. She said that her parents blamed her too, although I don't think that could be true. But you never know, it's possible. We barely see her side of the family these days. Anyway, I don't think she's ever going to get over it. This past six years or so it's just got worse as she shuts herself away from anyone but me. She's seen countless therapists, attended clinics. She hasn't held a job down for more than a few months - always off sick. And now she's often suicidal. So you see, my selfish side needed an escape. But at the same time, I *have* to support her.'

Victoria placed her hand on mine and gave me a sympathetic smile. 'You poor thing, I had no idea. That's an awful situation to be in. I'm hardly surprised you got involved with someone else. You must be emotionally drained.' She released my hand and raised her cup to her lips, before pausing and asking the question I'd been dreading. 'Do you love Sarah?'

I shrugged. 'I don't know, Vicky, I really don't.'

'Did you ever love her?'

'I'm sure I did. I didn't marry her out of sympathy. Back then she was... she *seemed*... much less affected by her sister's death. Maybe she was suppressing it and that's why she's falling apart now. Before I knew it I'd become so entangled in her problems, so sorry for her, so aware of her pain that I couldn't have considered leaving her. And now, I just don't know. I don't think I really know what love is. Is it staying where you're at for the other person's sake when you'd rather be somewhere else - with *someone* else? Not that it matters anyway. At least I know where I stand now. I've no reason to leave so I suppose I'll just have to put up with how things are.'

'But that's a life sentence, Tom! How long can you bear it? And this other woman - can we give her a name, by the way? - how do you know she won't change her mind, ask you to pick up the relationship again?'

I sighed and rested my chin on my clasped hands, elbows back on the table. 'Her name's Caroline. And no, she won't contact me again. It's over. Definitely over.'

'How can you be so sure? You obviously meant *something* to her?'

I shrugged again. 'Maybe I was just a fling. Whatever her reasons at the time, it doesn't change the fact that she and her husband are back together again. She heard that he was seeing someone else and I suppose it made her think. Made her realise what there was to lose. They've got two kids still at school. A nice house. And she knew of my concerns for Sarah.' I picked up my coffee and warmed my hands on the cup. 'So they've patched up their differences. And in a big way, too; she's just found out she's pregnant and she's absolutely delighted.' I drank a mouthful of the rapidly cooling coffee, glad that I had finally unburdened my woes.

'It's not yours, is it?' asked Victoria with concern.

I almost spat the coffee back into the cup. 'No, of course not,' I replied through a fit of coughing.

'How are you so certain?'

'I had a vasectomy, years ago. Sarah and I didn't want kids and with her mental state perhaps that's just as well. Although maybe children could have helped. I suppose we'll never know.'

'So she's back with hubby. But what if you bump into each other again? Won't that make things a little awkward?'

I leant back into my seat. 'No, they're moving away. He's taken a position up north, somewhere in the Lake District. She's going to pack up working and be a full-time mother again. At least, until the baby's off to school, I imagine. Caroline's always struck me as a career-minded sort of woman.'

'Oh? What does she do for a living?' asked Victoria.

'Didn't I mention? She's a GP. They both are.'

I looked out of the window at the passing traffic. My confession was coming to an end and I was beginning to feel calmer and more able to cope with the outside world. I even managed a faint smile. When I turned back to Victoria her face was pale and she looked like she was going to be sick. 'Victoria? Are you alright?'

Then she spoke, slowly, with a marked change of tone, almost as if she knew what was coming. 'What's *his* name?'

'It's Richard.'

'The surname?'

'Greenlaw. Caroline and Richard Greenlaw.'

Her face was contorted, teeth biting her bottom lip as if trying not to scream. She was holding a metal teaspoon in her hands, bending it in two as if it were made of plastic, her knuckles white with the effort. And anger. Her eyes were wild and the colour was rushing back into her face. I'd seen Victoria angry only once before, when someone in the lab had carelessly destroyed months of work, but this was much more intense. Her body was visibly shaking, almost convulsing. Her lips, which had been tightly pressed together to contain the emotion, parted enough to hiss, 'get me out of here, Tom, I need some air.'

'Victoria? What's the matter?'

She shot to her feet, knocking over her chair and drawing glances from the other customers. I caught her arm as she floundered first for her bag and then for direction and I guided her towards the door. We walked a dozen or so steps away from the café until she turned and slumped backwards against a wall. 'My legs are like jelly,' she said, 'hold me, Tom.'

We clung to each other like lovers. I wondered if passers-by were staring at us, although we were nothing exceptional, especially in Cambridge.

'What is it?' I asked again. She was staring down at the ground but when she lifted her head to look at me I saw that tears were now streaming down her cheeks. Then she began to sob; great racking sobs that shook us both. She stopped after a couple of minutes and drew in some deep breaths, wiping her eyes with the handkerchief I'd somehow found in my pocket whilst I was holding her.

Finally, she spoke: 'Richard Bloody Greenlaw is the man who was supposedly taking me to America. I didn't expect him to be taking his pregnant wife to the Lake District.'

'I'm sorry, Vicky, I'm so sorry. If I'd known, I wouldn't have dragged you through my problems.' I didn't know what else to say.

'No, I'm glad you told me. I ought to have guessed something was wrong,' she said. 'There have been so many nights recently when he's been unable to see me, without a particularly convincing reason. I feel so used. Why couldn't he have come clean about what was going on, instead of stringing me along like some lovesick teenager.'

I sighed and shrugged once more. It seems the Greenlaws had had their fun with the pair of us and were now skipping happily off into the sunset, leaving us beaten and broken in their wake. Victoria read my mind.

'We're in a right mess, aren't we, Tom?' At least she managed a wan smile. 'Where do we go from here?'

'Don't ask me difficult questions like that. I feel like I've been on auto-pilot for the past day or so and I'm not sure if I want to take back the controls. But I do know one thing: we can't stay here all day. There are some benches down by the river. Let's take a walk down there.'

Victoria nodded and smiled again. There was a momentary lull in the traffic and she took my arm as we crossed back over the road.

WINNING THE JACKPOT

by Val Woolley

'COME ON MAGGIE, hurry up or we'll not get decent seats.' Muriel Price poked her head round the front door. It was unlike Maggie to be late; usually she was ready and waiting in the porch. Muriel scanned the hall looking for signs of violence. Eddie had a reputation for knocking his wife about, although it was a long time since he had done so, but as Muriel thought to herself, a leopard rarely changes his spots.

Maggie saw her glance and interpreted it correctly. 'No Eddie's been fine since, well since; you know,' her voice tailed off, and they both remembered the night when Muriel had called round for a chat and found her friend in a heap on the floor. Maggie had refused to go to the hospital, and so Muriel's husband and a couple of fellow miners had taken Eddie behind the garages. Eddie had never touched her since, but he could make her life very difficult. It was after that incident that Muriel started to take Maggie to bingo with her on a Friday night, and Maggie loved it. Oh not the game itself, it was just the fact that she was out with a group of friends, sharing a laugh and a joke, and maybe a pizza or fish and chips afterwards.

There was a bar in the social club, but Maggie never drank anything stronger than lemonade, and Muriel and her friends drank coke or cider, preferring to spend their money on bingo specials and bonus tickets.

'Sorry I wasn't ready', Maggie whispered, as they entered the club, 'but I nipped up to the cash machine to get some money for tonight.' Muriel surmised correctly that Eddie had been pinching his beer money from his wife's purse again.

'Get another purse love, and just leave a small amount in the old one, and hide the new one,' she advised.

Maggie nodded, wondering if her friend knew everything that went on in her house. The Bingo hall at the local Working Men's club was already filling up by the time they got there.

'Quick Maggie, grab that seat, and save the one next to it for Babs.' Maggie put her bag on the next chair, just as a large woman made her way towards them, saw the seat was taken and hovered over the one next to it, before moving on to the next table.

'Flipping Heck, I thought 'Sit-Down-Irene' was going to take Bab's seat,' Muriel breathed.

'Why is she called Sit-Down-Irene?' Maggie asked.

'Because she always argues if she misses a number, and everyone shouts 'Sit down Irene' to her.'

Babs bustled in to join her friends, full of the news that there was going to be a national link up for the last game.

'Oohh I won a big Christmas turkey, last time they did that,' Muriel exclaimed.

They bought their tickets and settled down to a serious night's gaming. Muriel won £40 on a first line, and then the TV screen lit up and the big game of the night was ready to start. Clubs all over the country linked up for a game of bingo with literally hundreds of participants. The spot prize for their club went to the chair number of the woman sitting next to Babs.

'I should have been sitting there,' a voice called, 'That was my seat.'

'Sit down Irene!' the crowd yelled.

Sit-Down-Irene, sat down, still muttering that that had been her intended seat.

Then the silence descended as the final game started. Maggie had bought two tickets for it, but her friends had bought five each, and were concentrating intently on their cards. Suddenly Maggie realised she only wanted one more number to win.

'Five and nine, the Brighton Line', the caller on the TV screen called.

'Yes,' shouted Maggie.

'HOUSE' shouted her friends.

The steward came down and checked her card, then switching on his microphone he exclaimed, 'The lady is a winner.'

'Yes!' shouted Maggie's friends.

Maggie went home clutching her handbag containing a cheque for £9,576. Tomorrow she would open a bank account, but just for the night she left her handbag at Muriel's house. Muriel had promised to go to the bank with her in the morning.

As Maggie lay in bed that night listening to Ted snoring in the middle of the bed, she knew exactly what she was going to do with the money. Muriel (as promised) took her to the bank in the morning, and once the bank account had been opened, Maggie treated her friend to coffee and cake. Muriel sipped her milky latte, and then asked the question she had been dying to ask all morning.

'Well love what are you going to do with your winnings?' Maggie smiled at her, and Muriel realised it was the first proper smile she had ever seen on Maggie's face.

'Muriel, do you know how much it would cost to get a divorce?'

MEMORY BANK

by Anne Howkins

*T*HERE'S NOTHING LEFT, *they stole it all. They watched and planned their attack. They knew how to wheedle their way in, I had no defence. I was stalked, believe me, they knew how to get what they wanted — the precious stuff — and they just came and helped themselves. They sucked my memories away.*

I was at a loose end. The twins were away on their gap year travels; the decree absolute had arrived. At least Rob had had the decency to make a good settlement so money wasn't an issue. He'd asked me for some photos, so mum had suggested that she should help me sort out the over-flowing boxes lurking in the attic. It took months. You forget so much, then you pick up a dog-eared photo, and you're there again. Like that snap of the girls struggling to get into wetsuits the first time we took them surfing. Mum started laughing as soon as she picked it up. Then I reminded her about Rob getting stuck in his, and how he flapped around on the sand like a beached whale...all that flab disappeared once he met Veronica, as did the tracksuit bottoms and logo T-shirts. I laughed till I got hiccups, face streaked with tears and snot and every time mum caught my eye we'd start again. And then a rogue blood vessel in her head exploded.

After her stroke I used to sit with her for hours and just talk about those photos, tell her the family stories. The nurses used to encourage me, said she could hear. I didn't believe them, but at least it made me feel useful. She's a tough old bird, mum, they kept telling me she'd succumb quietly to an infection, but she just kept on breathing and dribbling. I used to have my lunch in the cafe next to her care home, and that's where I bumped into James.

We hugged and talked, drank coffee after coffee, flooded each other with words.

'Just like the old days, eh?'

Oh, he was a charmer, always made my stomach lurch and knees wobble with a sly glance from under impossibly long eyelashes. He knew he was beautiful and used his looks unashamedly. James always got what he wanted, and then got bored with his conquest very quickly. I'd never been able to meet his standards and kept my own lustful desires well hidden away — we were just mates as far as he was concerned.

'So you're happily married with a dozen gorgeous kids?' I smiled the words at him, giddy with the possibility of... well who knows?

'Lord no, tried it once, got a kid in the States, their mom bleeds me dry. You?'

James had this knack — nobody else but you mattered to him, he listened, asked the right questions, and he made you feel like a million dollars. I knew this. And it wasn't just about sex with James, he'd promise you the world, then snatch it all back when he got bored. So I was reticent. Just gave him the bare bones. But I did think I could talk to him about mum. He'd lost his mother from a stroke when we were at college — mine was the shoulder he used at her funeral. He took it all in. If he'd paid as much attention in lectures all those years ago he might have got his psychology degree, not gone off to be some sort of New Age counsellor.

'Lord, look at the time, I must get back to mum. This has been great, maybe do it again sometime?'

After exchanging phone numbers, his parting embrace was a little tighter than I expected, not that I was complaining. I couldn't remember the last time anyone other than my daughters had touched me with any real affection. Maybe mum noticed the animation in my voice as I told her about lunch; at least James was something new to talk to her about. It was only then that I realised that I'd not asked him about why he was in that cafe.

He didn't waste much time getting in touch. I agreed to meet him for lunch in a couple of days. Just enough time to keep me waiting without losing interest. After he'd called I took a long hard look at myself and didn't like what I saw. Hair like straw, scraped back in an elastic band. Jeans hanging off my gaunt hips, I looked like a bag lady. I tried on every single item of clothing I possessed, most of which went straight into black bin bags, too dire for the charity shop.

'Mum won't notice if you miss a morning,' I told myself, booked a haircut and dug out my credit card.

'Wow, you're looking great.' James pulled me into him, and kissed my neck, so, so gently.

I hardly dared speak, I'd flood the room with butterflies. So I let him get me a coffee and listened to him chat about college days. Eventually the Lepidoptera settled and I found my voice.

'So why are you here, now?'

'I'm doing some work with care homes. My organisation has done some really exciting projects working with old people and troubled youngsters.' His eyes glinted, he was more focused than I'd ever seen him, so I listened while he explained what they did.

'Can I check I understand this? You take the memories of people who've had happy family lives, and use those to show these difficult kids how families should work?'

'You got it, you always were a smart cookie.'

He was so plausible. All I'd have to do was give some interviews to his colleagues, prompted by family mementoes. If I was a suitable 'memory donor' then they'd want to hypnotise me — apparently this gave my stories more depth — and make recordings. Then they used hypnosis and some kind of behaviour therapy to implant the memories in a kid who'd had a rough time. By giving them a happy childhood, their future behaviour could be changed. The way James explained it, it was the way to get them away from a life of crime or worse. He gave me lots of leaflets to read, and information about their organisation.

'Check us out Carla, don't rely on what I'm telling you. This stuff is incredibly powerful, we're subject to all kinds of scrutiny, so you can trust us that it's all above board.' His voice was calm and very trustworthy.

I looked up the website. It was very technical, full of science with lots of cited research. There were names I recognised from my college days and they had lots of testimonials from youth workers and schools all over the world. The programme was called *Mending Memory*. I spent hours watching videos of kids who'd participated in the programme, it really did seem to change their behaviour.

'It sounds amazing mum, they take away the hurt from these poor kids. Give them a proper childhood. I know it's fake, but it's got to be better than their reality...' I rattled away to her about it for several days.

James had explained that he wouldn't work with me. I spent ages getting ready for the so called Memory Gatherer to visit me, looking through the photo albums, watching the cine films. Sarah explained the process, why it was better to be in my own home (I'd be more relaxed), that props would help and that I could stop the process at any time. I didn't notice the way she led the conversation, how she used key words to direct my thoughts, I just felt myself warm to her. This was something I could do to give other kids the same chances mine had, what harm could come of that?

'Hey Carla, here's some tea, you were so relaxed you dropped off.' Her voice seemed far away. 'This was a great session, you've given me some lovely memories. I'm going to leave you to rest now as the process can be quite tiring. I'll call you in a day or two to arrange another visit.'

I felt light headed and just sat there for a while, not really able to gather my thoughts. It was only the next day that I realised that I couldn't remember anything from the session with Sarah. Panicked, I called her. Perfectly normal she assured me, that's how all the donors felt. I began to feel reassured, it all appeared plausible. We could leave the next session for a couple of days if I wanted. And then she said they'd found a perfect recipient. A twelve year old who'd been in care for most of her life. She was one of those girls you read about in the paper; had been groomed by an Asian gang, but had been too scared to testify at their trial. Her psychologist felt she couldn't make any progress unless she could excise some of the terrible things that had been done to her. She'd been referred to their organisation. Sarah thought that some of my memories of bringing up the twins would help her. How could I not go on? I thought of my girls at twelve. They were riding ponies, learning to surf, piano lessons, just being kids. So we arranged for Sarah to visit me again.

It took me two days to recover from the next session. I'd never believed that someone could feel as if they'd been run over by a bus, but I did then. The only thing that got me out of bed was a call from the nursing home, asking me for a new nightie for mum. I called a taxi, too weak to drive, then I had to give him the card from my purse with the nursing home address. Every time I tried to speak my voice sounded as if I was in a tunnel and I couldn't say the right words. It was a strange journey, the sky seemed to be too low and the roads undulated as we drove along.

'Carla, are you OK? Sit down with your mum, I'll get you some water. We thought you might have been ill. Are you sure you should be here?'

I flopped down at mum's side. She looked odd. The nurse did too, their faces seemed to have been mixed up, a bit like Picasso's pictures. I couldn't remember the nurse's name. I'd tried to speak, but my words weren't right. Then the room dived away from me.

'Hey Carla, you're awake.' Someone helped me sip some water, propped me up. 'You're in St George's Hospital. I'm Ruth Carter, one of the doctors. How are you feeling?'

'What's happened to me?' my voice was thready, my mother's before her stroke.

It took ages for her to explain it, they thought I'd been drugged. There were some bruises inside my elbow, signs that I'd had something intravenously, but I'd not been treated in hospital or by my GP. I'd been delirious and then comatose. I'd been there for three days. I couldn't answer any of her questions, I couldn't remember anything other than mum being in the home.

They let me go home the next day. I kept feeling as if I'd lost something but I didn't know what. When I went to see mum, there was an album on her table — the first photographs were of a man with a woman and two girls on the beach. They were getting ready to go surfing. The neatly written caption said 'Carla, Rob and the girls. Cornwall, July 2006'.

I wondered who this other Carla was.

'Have you ever been surfing Kayleigh?'

She turns to James, already laughing.

'Dad, trying to get out of his wetsuit, he fell over….' and then she is holding her hand over her mouth, shoulders around her ears, and her laughter fills the room.

James turns to Sarah.

'It works…'

EAVESDROPPING

by Brenda Millhouse

THE LARGE THICK envelope dropped through the letterbox and landed with a thud on the communal hall floor. Eve had been watching for him, and before the postman had even reached the end of the path to continue on his round, had run downstairs to see if it was what she hoped it would be. The size and unfamiliar stamps brought a satisfied smile to her face; this must be it at last.

She had been planning this change in her life for months, ever since Aunt Amy had died and left the legacy which meant finance was no longer a problem. Hours of research on the internet had convinced her that she had chosen the very best. She would no longer have to accept the restrictions that circumstances had imposed for eighteen years, and could make something of her life.

The sun suddenly broke through the thin early morning mist and flooded the room with light. Eva looked out of the window again, but this time at the sea just a few hundred yards away which had turned from dull grey to an inviting shade of blue in an instant. It was far too nice to stay inside after a week of cloudy weather, and anyway, perhaps the sea air would help to get rid of the persistent cough which was all that remained of a summer cold of two weeks ago. She packed her small rucksack with the envelope, a can of coke and a beach mat, then set off for her favourite place in the dunes where she would be able to savour the life changing literature in private.

'Well, will you do it Wayne? I know you are perfectly capable of killing someone, you've bragged about it often enough, how you topped that security guard at Millers when he interrupted the robbery. There's five grand in it for you, two now and three when the job's done.'

'I'm not sure Pete, killing the mayor isn't exactly low profile is it? And why does it have to be at the official opening of the new cinema? Why can't I do it at his house, we all know where he lives? There's bound to be some decent stuff, I could make it look like a burglary.'

'I've told you, it's personal. That's where Marge works. I want the randy bastard dead and want as many people as possible to see him die, including Marge. Ok, I'll add another two grand to the final figure.'

'All right I'll do it. Have you got the gun? Careful, don't drop it in the sand! Shit! What was that? There's someone there!'

Detective Inspector Alan Munroe gazed down at the body of the young girl. She had lain undetected in a dip in the sand dunes until a dog being taken for an evening walk had alerted its owner with frantic barking.

'Single bullet wound to the heart, been dead between seven and eight hours,' said the pathologist in reply to the DI's questioning raised eyebrows. 'I'm tempted to say it looks like a professional job, but I'll leave the question to you of why anyone would want to shoot such an innocent respectable girl.'

The Inspector watched sadly as the paramedics zipped the body into the bag and stretchered it to the awaiting ambulance.

He bent and picked up the can of coke and glossy brochure that remained lying on the fine sand and read the blood spotted front cover: *Pittsburgh College for the Profoundly Deaf.*

THE SAT. NAV.

by Diane McClymont

Thank you for the sat. nav.
I know that you meant well
But it's causing us some problems
Which I'm about to tell.

My sat. nav. said, 'Turn left.'
My wife said, 'Wrong! Turn right'.
I did as she instructed
And we found the Isle of Wight.
The fact we wanted Brighton
Meant we were miles away
But dear wife still insisted
She preferred maps any day
To stupid, modern systems
Dictating which way to go.
I sighed and turned the car round,
Only seventy miles or so.

Last month we went to Scotland
And things were going fine,
'Turn right,' said the robotic voice.
'No, left,' said wife of mine.

It wasn't worth an argument
I did as she had said.
We'd booked a room in Edinburgh
But were Glasgow bound instead.

Now this is my dilemma
Please tell me what to do.
Do I send her on a map-reading course
Or give the sat. nav. back to you?

URBAN HUNTER

by Jackie Leitch

PATROLLING THE STREETS with agile grace, her instinct keeps her moving, keeps her searching. On the main roads it is never true night, street lights keep the darkness away, but there are always the murky alleyways and unlit paths for her to follow. Here, moving with stealth and care, she travels the little used byways deep in the heart of the city. Despite gleaming a lustrous silvery-blonde, she is all but invisible in the fleeting light.

Pausing, her keen sense of hearing catches a faint sound. There! Shoes scuffling on the tarmac, a whisper of movement; a sudden shout, quickly muffled; the sound of blows impacting on a body. She moves on; her green eyes focussed ahead, intent on her task. In the gloom, there's a body on the ground. Leaning over him, a predatory figure hunches and thrusts out a fist. Glimpsing the flash of a blade, she perceives danger. Moving more quickly, she lopes into the shadows. Tensing her muscles, she gathers her strength. With one fierce snarl she strikes.

On the ground, Rory's body trembles with shock and pain. He watches his attacker flee in fear. *'This can't be happening'*, he thinks, pressing hard on the wound in his neck.

Panting from the chase, his protector returns. She nudges him and then sees the blood pooling on the ground beside him. Her breath brushes his cheek as she curls up beside him, sharing her warmth and comfort, sharing her life force. Ensuring he will live.

Alerted by the noise, someone has rung the police: she can hear a siren approaching. It's time to go. For a moment, she stands over him, looking down, straight into his eyes. They reflect the pain and anxiety he feels, their brown depths shadowed with confusion; hers, a brilliant, sparkling green, glow clear and strong. A second later, she is gone.

Next day, sitting opposite the young policewoman, Rory insists that he was rescued by a wolf not a dog. He reiterates that he was conscious all through the attack and rescue, and was not hallucinating, despite the blood loss. As he speaks, he notices that the policewoman appears to believe him, unlike the officers at the scene the previous night who were openly sceptical. She is looking at him with encouragement and interest. He thinks she's beautiful, despite the ugly uniform. It occurs to him that he should ask her out for a drink.

She asks if he's still in pain, 'You seem to have made a quick recovery, though.'

He nods, 'Yeah, it is painful. I suppose I was lucky that wolf looked after me until the hospital could stitch me up. Although it's a bit hazy and I'm not sure exactly what happened. Anyway, whatever it was she did, it seems to have worked.

He looks upset, commenting, 'People like him - y'know, the bloke who attacked me - they're animals'.

'No.' She disagrees with him, her voice gentle. 'He was worse. Many animals who live in groups take care of each other.

She leans towards him, 'Do you fear being out alone now, Rory?'

He shrugs. 'I guess I do. Especially late at night. I just took a short-cut home, y'know? Bothering no one. I don't get it. Anyway, from now on I shall stick to the main roads, no more dark alleys for me.'

'Don't be fearful. It was a misadventure, and you were saved from harm.'

'Yeah. But. By a wolf? In the city? That's almost as scary as being assaulted.'

She looked at him, head on one side, 'They are very faithful – wolves. Protective and strong. They defend what is theirs. You are safe now.'

'Yeah, well. Don't get me wrong, Brigitte. I'm kinda glad she was there, but it's still a bit weird.'

She smiles, all business again. 'It must seem that way. Make a nice cuppa, shall I?' she asks, moving towards the kitchen.

Rory watches her, impressed by her lithe and graceful walk. *Yes,* he decides, *I will definitely ask her out.*

As she drops her cap onto a chair, her silver-blonde hair catches the light; for a moment it looks exactly the same colour as last night's she-wolf. As if she knows what he is thinking, Brigitte looks back at him, narrowing her green eyes slightly, and smiles again. 'Tea first and then we need to talk,' she says. 'Your life will be different now, so you have to know what to expect. But, I will be here to guide you, to protect and defend you. We're pack now.'

JESSIE'S LIE

By Joan Stephenson

JESSIE BECKETT'S HUSBAND, Peter, had sauntered off to the club bar, as he usually did on these occasions. An indifferent dinner had been cleared away, pompous speeches concluded and Jessie, who had never putted a ball in her life, was left at this table for ten with one empty chair and eight golfers.

It didn't bother her that she was out on a limb this evening. Rather more need to worry, she thought, if she had felt at home here at the club's annual ladies' night. No doubt Peter was making himself comfortable with some other group by now. He was a sociable chap and a good husband, so she didn't grudge him his freedom. They were content to hold each other on light reins. Later on, over cognac and bath olivers they would mull over their evening. He would feed her titbits of gossip and they would laugh quietly together.

Peter relished his club and sometimes Jessie wished she could do the same, but not often. This year she decided to be more tolerant of what would be the usual hour of ghastly entertainment.

Chandeliers dimmed, footlights blazed and the band blared off in crescendo. Rich plush curtains hiding a dais at the far end folded up and away. A handsome enough singer in an old-fashioned dinner jacket was announced with gusto. The audience clapped politely as he strode into the spotlight and swung into his repertoire of nostalgia.

Jessie glared at the golfers to shut them up. The songs were past their sell-by date, sickly with shallow sentiment but they conjured an era and she wanted to listen.

'Long ago and far away
I dreamed a dream one day...'

She forced the tears out of her eyes down into her nose. She would die if the golfers caught her weeping over such stuff. Nobody else in that room could be affected as much as she by that song.

She was back in a Derbyshire council school circa 1935 in the scholarship class. That year only two pupils had got through the arithmetic, English and intelligence tests with one more hurdle to go, the headmaster's report. Mick Macallum and Jessie, both ten years old, were interviewed together in the headmaster's study.

Mick was the cleverest child in the class. Nobody could touch him at mental arithmetic or anything else for that matter. He got the right answers out before the questions were finished and, not having an ounce of the swot in him, was the most popular boy in the class as well.

He and Jessie lived at opposite ends of the village but she knew his house almost as well as her own. Everybody was welcomed at the Macallum's. With such a large family, what did half a dozen more matter? Apart from children of all ages, their house was always full of noise and the crusty- yeasty smell of new bread.

Balm bread was Mrs. Macallum's speciality. Mick's father worked shifts so was sometimes home during the day. Mrs. Macallum in her cross-over pinny and Mr. Macallum in his shirt sleeves, together would cut and butter slice after slice, doling it out to ever growing queues of Mick's friends.

Jessie loved Mrs. Macallum's balm bread and she loved Mrs. Macallum. She also loved her own mother who was particular and kept a well-run house with strict rules but she had produced only two girls, criticized their friends and didn't make balm bread. Whenever Jessie knocked at the Macallums' door and heard the din within she couldn't help but make comparisons. It was such a gloriously cheerful din.

The headmaster asked them what they wanted to be when they grew up. Jessie was ready for this one. Her mother had primed her to say either a teacher, nurse or private secretary. She opted for the latter and the headmaster looked pleased.

'Private detective, Sir,' said Mick, sharp as a needle, eyes bright enough to light a taper and Jessie noticed a downward turn of the headmaster's mouth.

She moved on to Queen Elizabeth's Grammar School For Girls two miles away. Mick stayed at the village school and they rarely met after that. Mick went to chapel at his end of the village and Jessie went to church at hers. The war came and she stood in plenty of queues but never again in one for Mrs. Macallum's balm bread.

One golden afternoon, when they were both eighteen, they came face to face round the corner of Bolton's paper shop. Mick stopped short in a blaze of sunlight, his Pilot Officer's new blue uniform receding to grey, his eyes as lively as ever. Jessie stayed in the shadow of Bolton's sunblind. Its shade deepened the pattern of her pretty new dress run up from a length of curtain material by her clever mother.

There was a yard of pavement between them. They smiled at each other. Jessie thought he looked wonderful. They might have drawn closer, embraced, kissed even, but something, Jessie didn't know what, held her back. Mick sensed it, she knew. He was at the end of a short leave and she was going to a London teaching hospital to become a nurse. They hesitated, lingered a brief while and parted. The aged tenor ended on a long note,

'Just one look and then I knew

That all I longed for long ago was you.'

He was definitely off key but there was a thunderous round of applause. He made an exaggerated bow, flung his arms wide and exited to a roll of drums.

Quick as a cat, Jessie ran the length of the club room, on to the dais, to fumble between the thick red curtains.

The singer was backstage, breathing heavily. He looked done in. Over bright grease paint ran in streaks down his lined face. Jessie was shocked at the sight but she grabbed him by the arm.

'Please sing it again. Long Ago And Far Away. Please, you must.'

She sat through the second rendering of that song, her throat as tight as a miser's purse.

'Long ago and far away must have meant a great deal to you, Mrs. Beckett.' She looked up at a newly enrolled club member she hardly knew.

'May I?' He took the empty seat beside her. 'Will you tell me your story if I tell you mine?' She managed no more than a nod of assent.

He took me back to the war, to an R.A.F. station in Bedfordshire. Two young men, Mick and Chip, pilot and navigator, were called to the C.O.'s office. They were given a mission, highly secret and as highly dangerous. They were also given a forty eight hour pass and a piece of advice, 'Get yourselves up to town, have a damned good time, not too much booze and a damned good kip afterwards. You'll get your final brief before take-off. And keep your mouths shut.'

They spit and polished themselves up and strolled around Leicester Square like a couple of Verdant Greens. Chip found the nerve to approach a likely looking girl and got a look cold enough to freeze a kettle of boiling water for his cheek.

Mick laughed and said he knew where there was a girl from home and he was going off to find her.

'So long, see you back at camp. Good luck, chum.' Chip grinned and went to the pictures to see Rita Hayworth and Gene Kelly in 'Cover Girl' and yes, you've guessed it. The theme song was 'Long Ago and Far Away'.

Two days later they were flying over the Balkans with three human packages to be dropped off at an exact spot. Chip, the navigator, was apprehensive. The moon was high, the sky as bright as a ballroom. They would find their target easily enough but that same light made them vulnerable.

Mick was happy. Oh, yes, he'd found the girl from home; snatched her from the jaws of an old battle-axe. No, he didn't make it; didn't want to; hadn't even kissed her. They'd gone to a park, sat behind some sweet smelling bushes. She'd let him hold her hand. He was coming back to marry her.

He stopped shouting above the engine only to whistle or sing that song. It got on Chip's nerves a bit. The three agents, squatting uncomfortably in their cramped quarters, studied their watches and said nothing.

They completed their mission but were caught on the return hop. Chip ended up in a German prison camp. As for the agents, who knows? Mick was shot in cold blood just after he opened his chute. That was war.

It was a plainly told tale. No frills but startling enough to make Jessie unaware of the return stare of the golfers and the impression of Shirley Bassey centre stage.

'Now tell me yours,' Chip smiled and his eyes were warm. Jessie hesitated. She had a feeling of unutterable sadness. Not even Peter had heard her story.

She remembered that day all those years ago. She was on duty on the children's ward when the terrifying Sister Dorothy demanded her presence in the office. Sister Dorothy was built like a tank. Her uniform had a treble-starched look, stiff as armour plating. Small eyes of the brightest blue stared out of her brick red face like a pair of speedwells struggling through a clump of sorrel.

'Change into mufti, nurse and go into the quad. A young man is waiting,' she said. 'You may take the rest of the day off.' and for once in her life, she smiled.

Jessie knew if her mother had called, the answer would have been a firm refusal, but Sister Dorothy had been young once. So she said.

It was May time and warm. She slipped into her now faded curtain dress. She and Mick took the bus to Kew Gardens. The conductress punched their tickets while humming that song. Between long silences they held hands and reminisced behind the lilac bushes. The future hung like an iridescent bubble suspended between them. Nothing seemed permanent but Mick fell in love that afternoon. She would never forget the way he looked at her.

The gates were closing by the time they left the gardens and they went to a café for high tea. A wireless played that haunting melody. Notes tumbled from windows, hovered round doorways, dawdled between buildings. She thought how sentimental all their war songs were and how vigorous had been our fathers' Great War marching songs, while Mick's eyes never left her face.

Mick got her back to the hospital by eight o'clock, as Sister Dorothy had ordered. They lingered awhile, he in his blue uniform, she in her curtain frock, as they had done once before. Again there was the restraint of that indefinable something.

She never saw Mick again.

Her mother wrote to say he'd been killed in action. She knew that next time she went home she ought to see Mick's mother. Dear, warm hearted Mrs. Macallum would have opened her arms to Jessie. Drowning in self- deception she would have turned her and Mick into sweethearts and I couldn't bear the pretence.

She ignored the golfers, excused herself to Chip and went to look for her husband. Arm in arm they took the lift to their room, the tray of cognac and Bath Olivers already ordered. Peter handed her a glass.

'I saw you engrossed with that new chap, Chip what's-is-name so I didn't interrupt. You were very tête-à-tête. What was he on about?'

'Oh, this and that, nothing really.' And Peter believed her as she set down her glass to give him a kiss and a hug, their future secure and her rose coloured spectacles firmly fixed.

That had been her mother's advice the night before their wedding.

'They'll slip sometimes,' she said, 'but never ever take them off. And don't hark back.'

OVER THE TOP

by Linda Cooper

I'M IN THE garden killing a cabbage. One of the things I love about gardening is the opportunity to vent frustrations and behave violently without involving the law. Mind you, right now I'm rapidly beginning to wonder if I should call the police to search for my wife who's been missing since this morning. Where the hell is she?

The slaughtered cabbage is dark green, crisp and pungent. Ideal accompaniment for a roast dinner should anyone be available to prepare it. My stomach and the fridge are empty and much as I love to grow edible produce, I have no idea how to cook it and no inclination to learn. That's her department, or at least it was until recently.

In theory retiring to the coast seemed a good move and I hoped it would give her a new lease of life. The temperate climate and rich soil are ideal for my horticultural passion and I secretly nursed the idea she'd become interested and involved. Experience should have warned me there'd be as much chance of that as world peace, but I'm ever the optimist. If I caved in to reality life would be unbearable apart from my garden. A rare haven for sensory delight and inner peace. In truth I have more affection for the carrots I've just pulled than my wife.

Serves me right really for rushing things. I should have looked around for a more compatible partner instead of getting hitched to the first woman who showed an interest. But things were tolerable while she stuck to her side of the bargain, leaving me to mine. Her life of domestics, soaps and trivia hardly makes for an exciting partner, but at least it ensured my dinner was on the table, my socks in pairs and conversation kept to a minimum. But now, after all these years she's started behaving strangely and I can't figure out why.

It's almost dark when I hear the click of her key in the lock. She bursts into the lounge smiling like a demented clown, wearing an expression I'd only associate with a teenager high on crack, a lottery winner or post coital ecstasy. I know none of those are the reason for her smug countenance as she's too cautious to indulge in anything mood altering, too frugal to purchase a lottery ticket and too damned ugly to attract any admirers. She's a dumpy woman with thin lips and thick glasses.

'Where on earth have you been until this time? I'm starving and you've not done any shopping.' Not the most subtle approach I know, but I'm weary of her recent furtiveness.

'Oh don't start, Gerald. You and your stomach. What do you care anyway?'

Hostility and the distinct odour of stale sweat linger in the air. She's obviously been exerting herself in some way, which is totally out of character. She generally has the vitality and intellect of a geriatric slug.

'You could have phoned. I was worried about you,' I lie.

'That would be a first. Anyway, my phone's dead. It needs recharging.'

'Why? You hardly ever use it.'

'Well I do now.'

'What's going on with you? You're out all hours, nothing gets done at home and now it seems you're always on the phone.'

She hesitates then sighs, averting her narrow eyes. 'If you really want to know I've started geocaching.'

'Geo what?'

'I'm too tired to explain and I doubt you'd be interested anyway. Look it up on the internet if you really want to know. I'm going to bed.' Her face resumes its agitated, squinty look. I guess I burst her bubble and will be penalised for it tomorrow.

The door slams and I'm reduced to making a sandwich. Later I can't resist the temptation of checking out what it is that's distracting my wife from her duties. Turns out this geocaching business has been going on for years. It's some sort of treasure hunting game where you use a GPS to search for containers hidden all over the world. When you find one you have to sign a logbook inside the container then log it on the website later. Well, Whoop-de-do. What a bloody waste of time.

Things deteriorate over the next few weeks. I'm forced to spend more time harvesting salad crops as the wife's rarely available to cook. Weight is dropping off me without any decent meals and my unwashed clothes are too large. The dirty house is in chaos and I'm rapidly reaching the end of my rope. I know I wanted her to develop an interest in something, but this geocaching racket has turned into an obsession. Completely over the top.

Today she even threatened to have the garden slabbed if I don't stop complaining. In order to pacify her I've had to agree to take her out in the car tonight to find one of the blessed caches. She had to give up driving a few years ago when her myopia took a turn for the worse. Turns out this geocache can only be hunted out in darkness as it's reflective and can't be seen in daylight. I've not seen her this excited since the last time I bought her a new cooker. Maybe she'll even use it once she's logged her latest find.

'It's up on the downs near that monument. I reckon it's hidden in a tree stump,' she relays enthusiastically as I drive with gritted teeth and a rumbling belly. 'You can walk behind me and read the instructions while I use the map on my phone.' I've never felt so underwhelmed.

I park the car and she heads out into the darkness with her flashlight and phone. There's a hint of autumn in the air and I button my coat against the chill wind. I trail behind her praying she'll locate the stupid geocache quickly so we can get home for some dinner.

'How many metres north of the monument is it?' Her voice echoes in the misty, evening air. 'I can't see the phone very well. Just check the instructions will you? Is it twenty?'

I hold my torch over the paper. A thought pops into my head. It's pure evil, but my mouth takes control before I can stop it. 'No, it's thirty metres.'

It's quiet for a few minutes then her voice again, fainter, more indistinct. 'Are you sure? I thought...'

A screech fills the air, reminiscent of a cat on helium, followed by a distant thud and then silence.

By the time an ambulance arrives the tide has come in and the body been washed away from the rocky beach where she fell from the cliff's edge. An attractive female police officer drives me home in my car as she's concerned I might be too shocked and upset after such an awful accident. I'm reduced to making a sandwich again.

A few weeks later the same police officer drops by to inform me they're calling off the hunt for my wife's body as the seas are rough at this time of year and there's little hope of discovering it now. We get chatting over tea and fig rolls and she tells me she understands how devastated I feel as she lost her husband a couple of years ago. She confides she's about to retire from the police service and is contemplating securing an allotment to work on during her free time.

'Tell you what,' she says. 'I can see you're not looking after yourself too well, so how about we go and dig up some of those beautiful home grown vegetables out there and I'll rustle you up a decent meal.'

Bingo. A good looking widow with twenty-twenty vision, plus a love of gardening and cooking. If I decide to search for a replacement I'll be a lot more careful this time, but it's looking promising. A step in the right direction if you'll excuse the pun.

THE REUNION

by N.K. Rowe

WELL, I *KNOW* I said it'd never happen, but one day you're a cocky bugger fêted by music journalists across the Western world and the next you wake up on your fiftieth birthday wondering where the last twenty years went.

I'd been at some friend of a friend's party and Dave, the drummer, was there; I don't know if he knew someone or had just blagged his way in. But that put me, well, both of us really, in a bit of a bind. 'Cos you face the prospect of pretending you don't know he's there (which makes you look like a complete dickhead) or engaging in an awkward conversation (which, being English blokes, is excruciating – you'd rather put your head down the toilet than seek out that kind of social interaction). Or, and this is the favoured option, acknowledging him with a nod which is intended to be seen by as many other people as possible so they can stop bleeding well gossiping about you both.

There was a girl there that I was chatting to – yeah, 'to', not 'up'; she was only about twenty and didn't know me from Adam – and when she heard I'd been in a band she only goes and digs him out of the crowd and pushes him over to me, asking if we'd ever met. Dave's rolling his eyes and indicating that she's not the smartest cookie in the packet, so of course I said 'no, who is he?'

We then had a brilliant hour or so, playing on her innocence, pretending not to know each other while she's asking questions about our other band members. I told her that my drummer was a semi-literate ape with all the creative talent of a dead sheep while he said that his guitarist was a spaced-out junkie who can barely string two words together. So, in a somewhat unorthodox fashion, we broached the sensitive subjects of his terrible solo album and my period of phenomenal drug abuse that ultimately ended the band. For the record, we agreed that our respective lead singers were tasteless narcissists and our bass players were both under-rated musicians who just happened to be bi-polar psychopaths.

We ended up ditching the party and the girl – actually I think she wandered off because we were ignoring her – and went back to Dave's gaff for a cuppa (yeah, woo, rock and roll). Turns out his sister had died – car accident – a couple of years ago. I felt terrible 'cos she was a lovely lass and I hadn't heard. But he had heard about my parents (cancer and heart attack) but hadn't known if I wanted to hear from him, or for him to go to the funerals. I told him he always was a soft sod, of course I would've wanted him there. But I understood why he was reluctant; in my worst days of druggie hell I was a vicious, opinionated tosser who had empathy for no-one and sympathy for no-one but me.

We sat there, in his unremarkable kitchen, with two mis-matched mugs of tea. And we cried. I don't think I've ever cried in front of a mate before, apart from family funerals and, you know, when Wigan won the FA Cup.

So it got us thinking about who we are now and who we were then, back when we were playing together. Turns out not only have I got clean, but Dave isn't the cultural wasteland we always thought he was; he only went a got a bloody degree in

Music History. I mean, OK, it's not actually composing or anything, but you should hear his critique of African rhythmic influences on early jazz. 'So, hang on,' we thought, 'if we've changed, what about Seb and Tez?'

Turns out our psychotic bassist was now a chilled-out session and club musician – with a bloody vineyard in France. And Seb was, as far as we could see, still Seb. He'd been on some reality TV show on ITV2 or something, not even Channel 5. I didn't watch it and he left after a couple of weeks. I don't know if he was voted out or just walked away – probably even odds on both options 'cos firstly he's an acquired taste and secondly he's a law unto himself. Which made us wonder whether he'd even consider the possibility of getting the band back together, even if for just some private jamming.

In the end it was Tez that made the surprising phone call to me; Seb had been staying at his French gaff for a few weeks during the past couple of summers and, having heard that me and Dave were knocking about Manchester together, they wondered whether we would be willing to have 'a bit of a reunion'. I think Seb's finances are not great so maybe the prospect of a sell-out reunion tour wasn't looking like the great betrayal of his principles that he always said it would be.

So before we knew it we were heading out to some practice rooms near Chester. We all arrived separately but, incredibly, *within an hour of the pre-arranged time*, which was completely unheard of – we used to be able to miss meeting times by weeks, never mind minutes. We dumped our gear and then went to the pub because the first rule of overcoming awkwardness is to have a pint. Except I'm on apple juice these days and Tez has wine and Dave prefers a well-aged whisky. I can't remember what the hell Seb drinks now; probably virgin goat's milk and royal jelly smoothie.

By the time we got back to the practice room and got set up it was gone midnight but we used to produce our best sessions in that timeless dark hole between one and five in the morning. We'd nearly finished tuning up when Dave started pounding out a beat. Tez joined in with a distinctive groove and suddenly we were into the first song we'd played together in two decades. The last time on stage we couldn't bear to look at each other. But this was how it always should have been; four mates, a bit greyer and balder and fatter but together and grinning like idiots. Except, after twenty bloody years, we weren't idiots any more.

JUST REWARD

by Theresa Richmond

HE FINISHED BRUSHING his teeth to the count of 100 for the top and 100 for the bottom. His tongue did the final check and glided home. Good, strong white teeth.

Just asking to be knocked out

A final flick of the heavy fringe that fell across his eyes, a last mechanical tug at his tie.

Let me pull that a bit tighter for you dick-head.

He left the bag with his games kit on the floor.

Games day is it? We know a game you'd like farm-boy...

The big holdall.

He'd need that today.

What you got in your bag today Boyzy Woyzy?

He quietly pulled it out from under the bed. Downstairs the door banged shut. His father had left to feed the beast.

Bloody mother's done a runner! Can't blame her. I mean, who'd want to wash his shitty pants?

No sound.

'There's just this letter to go out to Governors today, oh and the Parents Evening letters too if you can? You've done them already? Brilliant! You're ahead of me!' The Head Teacher went back to his pile of post by the window in the school office.

'Delivery, love!'

The Secretary pressed the button to let the deliveryman in.

'Sign 'ere. Where do you want them?'

'Thank you, can you stack them against the wall, we don't want someone tripping over and killing themselves.' She opened the spare key cupboard and picked out the store key.

One of the other keys was missing.

'Anyone seen the hall key? Doesn't seem to be here.'

'Didn't that boy from Year 10 need it late yesterday? Came back for his coat — thought he'd left it in there?'

He took two bites from the cold toast his father had left, pulled the zip on the holdall and lifted the heavy weight onto his shoulder.

Look at him - can't even lift his bag up. Bloody girl!

He caught his reflection in the mirror and noticed an odd upturn at the corners of his mouth.

What do you think you're smiling at fat face?

Behind him he could see that he'd left the glass door to the long wall cupboard open. When his father came back he would notice the gap that had been left, so he closed it and locked it again, returning the key to its place in the dust on top, where it had always lived.

He had to go through the front door sideways on because of the big holdall.

He would walk today, no bike.

Don't forget to tuck your trousers in, don't want them getting caught in your stabilizers!

He wanted to be late.

The strap of the holdall bit into his shoulder, the weight making him lean slightly to one side.

Out of the farm drive, along the lane.

No-one about.

Look! He's all alone. Nobody want to hold your hand today.....? They know where it's been.

He took his time.

He wanted to be sure they would all be in the hall by the time he arrived.

Bugger off and find another chair, no wankers in this row.

In his pocket, his fingers pressed against the cold metal of the key.

He was nearly there.

The hall was full. Row upon row of disinterested youth. They stood as the Head came to the stage.

'Good morning boys.'

'Good morning Mr. Hacker.'

'Our assembly this morning is about Just Rewards. Hands together.'

There was no warning.

The car came round the bend too fast.

It caught the holdall and sent him spinning high up towards the sunlight.

BLUE EYED GIRL

by Anne Howkins

A WE-STRUCK — THAT'S the only way I can describe how I felt when she arrived. She turned a couple into a family. We'd spend hours watching this tiny scrap of a person. Funny that she never held your gaze — huge azure eyes looked past you, finding something more interesting elsewhere. But she met her growth targets, ticking the boxes on the health visitor's endless reports in all the right places, so we were happy.

'I just wish,' sometimes I'd say to Steve 'that she'd smile a bit more.' He'd tell me she was fine; there was 'nothing to worry about.' And he'd go off to work and leave us to our day.

She was cooed over in her buggy, those luminous eyes like a flame to moths. She didn't smile at her admirers, in fact she didn't seem to notice them. She hated bright childish things, but was entranced by the big interactive sculptures in that South Bank gallery.

Once she was mobile she always crawled away from me. The moment I put her down she'd be off, as far as she could get. Looking for something. Once she spent a whole day watching a spider making a web, screamed when I tried to put her to bed for her nap.

'She'll be an explorer,' we joked, proud of our independent girl.

The health visitor suggested the mother and baby group in the church hall.

'Get you both socialising a bit.'

'I take her out every day. We go to all sorts of places. The park, museums, galleries...'

'Yes dear, but she needs to learn to be with other little ones. And it will do you good to meet other mums.'

Steve said I should go, get over my snobbishness. We argued, then I gave in. One afternoon a week would be bearable.

I did try, I really did. But she hated it. She screamed every time another toddler came near, and shuffled herself off as fast as she could. The trouble was, she didn't come to me. Just took herself under a table and glared at the other kids. And the other mums stared at me, disdain and pity on each face.

We went back to our routine of galleries and museums. We both felt safer. Her first word was 'Tate'. Not that she spoke much — she hummed a lot. Screamed a lot too. She would spend hours drawing. The crayon had to be sharp, as soon as the tip softened she would hurl it across the room. She never drew people or faces. No rainbow happy family pictures brightened our fridge.

Steve's niece was six months older. Her fourth birthday party was at one of those indoor play places. I told him she'd hate it. Another argument. I lost. We piled into the car, off to do what normal families do every weekend, bearing prettily wrapped bits of plastic and forced smiles.

Steve didn't speak a word on the journey home. 'Welcome to my world' I thought. That night's row reached a new peak, or maybe I should say low. He was convinced my lack of mothering had damaged his precious little girl, turned her against her daddy, ruined our perfect little family.

Then, before we could mend bridges, he packed a bag — he wanted some space. Funnily enough the 'space' was a blonde glamour model.

So we plodded on, just the two of us, living side by side in our own little world. Until the first day of school. Suddenly professionals were offering opinions, statements, specialist support. It wasn't just me and her any more. Neither of us liked the new arrangements.

While she was out I would pace the house, I couldn't settle to anything. Art lost its appeal, I needed her with me, staring and absorbing, ready to pour it all out onto paper as soon as we got home. Walking her home from school was an act of endurance. We'd wait until the other kids had frolicked off with their mums, spilling their day excitedly, wallowing in maternal love and pride. She'd walk stiffly behind me, always two paces back, arms clamped to her side, blue lasers boring my exhausted back.

Then, one dank December Sunday afternoon, the game started.

Instead of sitting on the sofa and trying to read while she lost herself in drawing the curved form that held her captive on that morning's outing, I lay on the floor. A human star, lost in space.

I felt her stop her measured hand movements, lift her eyes to me, and watch silently. I hardly dared breathe. This was more attention than she'd given me her whole life.

A century passed. Then she was standing astride me, lapis eyes scanning, the way she'd looked at the stone form that morning. My chest tightened. Then she sat on me, knees wedged into my arm pits, arms dangling by her sides. She bent her head further and contemplated my face.

Another century. I inched my arms towards her till they enfolded her skinny legs.

'I love you.' I whispered.

She stared at the rivers streaming down my neck. She touched my face. She raised her hand, staring at her wet fingers. Then she bunched her fingertips and put them to her mouth.

'Love' she said, softness for once in those sapphire orbs.

And so our game gave me scraps of sustenance. It had to be played on her terms, sometimes it would be weeks before she'd whisper 'Love' without raising her head. I'd stretch out on the floor and she'd sit on me. On a good day she would lean forward and allow her lips to feel salt on my skin.

Until the day I couldn't cry. Another dark December afternoon, it may have been Christmas, but not in our house — decorations sent her into a frenzied rage. We'd had a bad few weeks after she'd changed schools and had withdrawn even further. She wouldn't go into the galleries. Solidified in door ways, eyes tightly shut, arms clamped to her sides. The experts were pessimistic, they could offer only one solution. It would give me freedom, but none for her.

I lay down as she asked and let her weight sink into me. She lowered her head and gazed, looking for wetness. My face stayed dry — I was cried out. But she knew how to bring tears. She pinched and punched; bit and scratched; thumped and jumped. When I came round she was back at her table, making those infernal measured strokes.

I tried, I really did. I lay on the floor, day after day. The game was over, she made that very clear. Again the experts tried to persuade me, told me I could have my life back. They didn't seem to understand that she was my life.

So I found a solution.

It was easy to get her to drink the cloudy blackcurrant juice — she'd never paid any attention to how anything tasted and I'd deliberately added more salt to her supper , so she'd be thirsty. I swallowed mine in one gulp.

Now I wait, feeling the familiar carpet scratch my flesh. Limbs splayed I gaze at the ceiling.

She's stopped her drawing and staggers across the room to me.

Awkwardly she finds her familiar pose. 'Love' she slurs, 'love.' She leans forward, stiff arms either side of my shoulders till they can't take her weight any longer and she flops forward. Her forehead rests on the floor, our cheeks together. I wrap my arms around her and turn her wet face to mine and finally stare into that mesmeric blue.

Our breathing synchronizes and then the effort becomes impossible...

PARALLEL WORLD

by Brenda Millhouse

WHEN I'M MISSING you the most that's when I retreat into my, our, parallel world. The one that would have existed IF. It's the world where we are together, always have been, and always will be. A world that the power of reality can never destroy.

We met years ago, by chance, and were instantly attracted to one another. The chemistry was immediate but as we got to know each other an even deeper bond grew. One of trust, respect and close friendship, none of which have faded with the passing of time. Our courtship was bliss, our marriage a love match - everyone said so. We both worked hard to achieve our joint aim of a comfortable life, but because it was for each other, the occasional hardships were borne with no resentment. We enjoyed life, but most of all we enjoyed each other.

I have a picture in my mind of where we live now. A roomy but not pretentious house. Filled with the mementoes of a contented fulfilled lifetime together. Framed photos of the two of us in the places in the world that we both wanted to see together. The Great Barrier Reef, Japan, the Rocky Mountains. That was before the children came along. Two I think, a boy and a girl. It's difficult to imagine exactly what they would look like. I picture our son as tall like you. Our daughter is smaller, with my blond hair, but your striking blue eyes, and she adores you. They are both kind, honest and caring, but with a sense of adventure and purpose, for that is the example they have been set all their lives. They are becoming less dependent now with lives of their own, but we are still their best friends and confidants when they need us to be. Both of them sometimes embarrassed that their parents are still so obviously in love, but inside proud that's the way it is, and wanting the same for themselves one day. Naturally we wouldn't be without them, for they are our own creation, evidence of our combined existence. But we both revel in the extra time we have for just ourselves again. The house is filled with happiness too; you can feel it as you walk in the door. A house that is loved as much as the occupants love each other.

There are animals of course, we both love them. They provide such an easy way to teach your offspring humility and responsibility. Two cats and a dog at the moment who, although not spoilt, share in the warmth and love that our household radiates. The garden I have created is a delight all the year round. You hate gardening, but admire it all the same for my sake. In the summer we can entertain out there, but our house is a popular place to visit at any time of the year. Guests leave with a piece of our happiness, but then we have plenty to spare.

Right now I'm cooking you a meal, one of your favourites. Steak with all the trimmings, then rhubarb crumble to follow. The children are away with friends for the night, so after our meal and a relaxing time when we can both unwind (especially you, for your days are so long), we will go early to bed. Then we will make love with as much passion as we have from the start. Possibly more, for we have had more than twenty years of practice learning to please each other and both of us still take great delight and pleasure in doing just that.

I hear your car in the drive. It seems an age since you left early this morning and we kissed each other goodbye, as we always do whatever time it is. You will walk in the door put down your briefcase and hang up your coat. Then you will be there smiling at me, giving me a hug, and at last kissing me hello. That's when I open my eyes, and you're not here.

DIAMONDS ARE A GIRL'S BEST FRIEND

by Diane McClymont

THE APPLE PIE was perfect. They wouldn't be able to resist it, thought Snow White, as she placed it in the centre of the table. For once, her scheming cruel step-mother had come in useful. Snow White had recognised her straight away when she came calling that morning. The pathetic old-woman disguise hadn't fooled *her* and she had guessed that the rosy red apple her stepmother had offered her would be full of deadly poison. So having pretended to take a fatal bite she had collapsed onto the floor and the old hag had gone away happy.

Now, *that* apple was inside her beautiful pies. Not that she wanted to kill them (although the thought had often crossed her mind), just drug them for long enough so that she could nip to the mine and fill a bag with top quality diamonds. She deserved it after slaving away day after day for seven extremely ungrateful little men. Never a penny had they offered her. She was sick and fed up with their annoying idiosyncrasies; sneezing, grumbling, giggling...

She was leaving. She, Snow White, was going to paint the town red.

THE LUCKY SILVER THRU'PENNY

by Jackie Leitch

KATE SETTLED THE cardboard box in place and slammed the boot shut. *That was a bargain,* she thought. The car was cold and so was she, after spending a couple of hours rummaging through the amazing variety of things at the car boot sale. She turned the heater up high and soon began to thaw out.

Once home, she called out to her husband, 'Tom, come and see what I've got.' She took the cardboard box into the kitchen and opened it, careful of the fragile items it contained. Inside was a beautiful Victorian mixing bowl decorated with trailing vines, flowers and birds on the outside, and a narrow pattern repeated just below the rim inside.

'Look, Tom, isn't it lovely? It's china, see, not earthenware and it's in really good condition. Someone has cherished this and looked after it.'

'Yeah, nice.'

Next out were three plain pudding bowls of a more everyday sort.

'They're dull', said Tom.

'Yes, but they'll come in handy', replied Kate.

When she had taken out the four bowls Kate realised there was something else in the box. Lifting it out gently, she read '*Family Recipes*'.

'Oh, Tom, look. It's really old.'

But Tom had wandered away, back to his newspaper.

She stroked the faded material. Along one corner the pattern had disappeared almost completely and the edges were frayed where it had been opened over and over again. Inside, there were pages of handwritten recipes dating back to the 17th century, each beautifully written by many different hands. '*Alys's Roast Goose and Gooseberry Preserve Stuffing, 1696*'; '*Mrs Pothecary's Strawberry Fool, 1801*', and many more. Towards the end, she found a recipe for '*Mother's Special Christmas Pudding 1852*'. She found herself moved by the thought of the book being lovingly put together; generation after generation of women from the same family, each one contributing her favourite, and each recipe used over and over again throughout the centuries. *It's Stir-Up Sunday this weekend,* she thought. *I'm going to use the recipe from 1862 to make my pudding this year. See what it's like.* As the thought crossed her mind, a cold shiver ran down her back. She made a mental note to remind Tom to sort out the window; there was a definite draft in the kitchen. As she turned away, she thought she saw a flicker of white at the utmost edge of her peripheral sight. *And an appointment with the opticians as well* she decided.

The mixture was rich and dark. Kate stirred it up in the pretty Victorian bowl, standing at her kitchen table. She had been inspired by the name of the recipe to find her own mother's apron, tucked away as a keepsake, two years previously. It was thin and worn but Kate felt comfortable in it. Despite accepting the fact that she would never have children herself, there were times like this, stirring the Christmas pudding, when it still had the power to hurt. Putting the wooden spoon down, she wiped her hands on a cloth, ready to start transferring the mixture into the prepared greased bowls. She paused. *I've forgotten something*, she thought, dropping her hands to her sides and looking around the room. Again, there was an impression of movement and she frowned, distracted for a moment from the feeling that she was missing something important from the pudding.

'The silver thru'penny'. A small cool hand slid into Kate's and a thin coin dropped into the pudding mixture.

'Stir it in. You must stir it in. It brings good luck to those that find it. You make a wish and it comes true.'

Kate looked down. A small girl with soft, curling brown hair stood looking up expectantly. She looked an old-fashioned little creature, with her pretty white pinafore dress and a bow holding back her ringlets.

'Stir it in,' she repeated.

'Whose little girl are you? What are you doing here?' Kate said.

The child looked up at Kate, her face grave, 'My mother made puddings at Christmas, just like you. We always had a silver thru'penny in the pudding.'

Kate frowned, perplexed by the child and her story. 'But, how did you get here?'

'That is my mother's bowl you are mixing your pudding in and my mother's book you are using. I came with *them*. She loved the book and promised it would be mine when I grew up and married. But, I did not.'

Kate knelt and took the child's other hand, 'What happened, sweetheart?' she said.

'My mother died.' Kate felt the child's hands tighten in hers.

'Oh, you poor little thing. How did your mother die?'

'Mother died from taking too much laudanum.'

Kate paused a moment, *laudanum?* she thought, then focussed again on the child.

'Why was she taking laudanum?'

'She was sad because I had the silver thru'penny in my piece of pudding. Laudanum made her forget.'

Kate repeated, 'But, I don't understand. You found the coin, which you say brings good luck. What happened? Why didn't you marry and inherit her book?'

'Because Mother took the laudanum after I choked on the silver thru'penny *she* had put in the Christmas pudding.'

The child looked at Kate, drawing her closer. Her blue eyes grew darker and more intense. 'I cannot find her and I am lonely without my mother,' she said in a whisper. 'I can be your little girl if you wish.'

VICIOUS CIRCLE

by Kirsty Adlard

I CAN RECALL IT still. The balmy scent of lilac weighting the air, the Spring breeze lifting my cotton skirt in an intoxication of bare legs and promise. He held my hand lovingly — my right hand, I remember, not the one on which the previous evening he had slipped the carved ivory ring. Anyone could have a conventional solitaire diamond, I had told myself. Only a very special person chooses to give such an unusual token of love.

They were heavenly months together — long warm days and even longer passionate nights. Never had there been such a romance — or so I thought, all those years ago. He courted me with such gentleness and understanding, such patience and restraint. I blossomed like the rose on my delicate ring and gave myself gladly and with complete abandon.

I never did find the small portion of ivory which detached itself as he wrenched the ring from my finger. Perhaps that was unfortunate, though I could never have brought myself to repair it and wear it again, of course. Even to study the intricate carving now, at a distance of thirty years, brings back too many painful memories. I try to resist the temptation to retrieve it from its hiding place in the depths of my jewellery box.

How could he have treated me as he did — how could I have been so gullible? Those were the days before 'relationships'; it was marriage or nothing at all. Parents closed their ears to the idea of pregnancy outside marriage and their minds to the possibility of scandal. I still feel my colour rise at the remembrance of breaking that news; first to my parents, and then to him. I recall with clarity his expression, the sharp click as the ivory snapped — a portion bouncing across the room and disappearing — just as he did.

My daughter more than compensated for my loss of a lover she seemed to sense the unique part she played in my life. The void that was left when she, in turn, deserted me. Only now, in the long dark nights when sleep eludes me, do I find myself drawn to examine again that delicate carving and handle what had once been a perfect circle of ivory.

BROWNIE POINTS

By Linda Cooper

I bought a humble residence on the outskirts of the town.
A tidy little property; brand new, two-up two-down,
Nestling in a shady suburb, we'd be happy here for sure,
And life *was* hunky-dory until the Browns moved in next door.

They drew up in their Jaguar, it glistened in the sun.
My Lada looked inferior, something must be done.
At the showroom I decided on a Mercedes Estate,
With trendy tinted windows and personalised number plate.

Their caravan arrived next day, a very swish affair.
For them to own things we don't have just seems so damned unfair.
So now I have a motor home and I bought a boat as well.
There's no water for a hundred miles, but it's flash, so what the hell?

The Browns ripped out their windows, it really was amazing,
How quickly they replaced them, complete with triple glazing.
So of course we had to follow suit and now our new exterior,
With stained-glass leaded windows is looking far superior.

The Browns employed some builders; it filled me with dismay,
To see their home extended, I must take action right away.
So now we've a conservatory, four bedrooms and two showers.
The Browns may have a big house, but it's not as big as ours.

The Browns have two smart children; they go to private school,
Being a compact family suddenly feels uncool.
We only have the one boy; we hadn't planned on more,
But now we've had to breed again so we've got two-point-four.

The Browns have ordered satellite; there's a dish high on their wall.
We only have five stations so we can't compete at all.
But now we're having digital, ninety channels, interaction,
And I'm watching my new plasma screen with a smile of satisfaction

The Browns installed some decking and two massive water features,
They've created a gigantic pond and filled it full of creatures.
So I've been on the internet and bought my own reptile.
And now I have to make a sign 'Beware the Crocodile.'

The Browns built a pagoda, an arbour and a shed,
A tree-house for the children and a weed-free flower bed.
So we've had to do the same as them, but of course we've added
more.
It's taken every inch of space but we can still squeeze through the
door.

My bank keeps making phone calls; there's a loan shark on the
street.
If I don't pay my debts off soon I could wind up dead meat.
But money doesn't matter; one-upmanship's the game,
To get one over on the Browns my one and only aim.

Lately it's been very quiet; there's been no activity,
Perhaps the Browns have realised they cannot better me.
I'm feeling quite exhausted and a little bit perplexed.
But I'm ready for the challenge of whatever they do next.

Today it says 'For Sale' outside the house next door to mine.
The property stands empty; of Mr Brown there is no sign.
I thought I'd won the battle but nothing's fair in life.
Because this morning I discovered he's absconded with my wife.

LATE

by N.K.Rowe

M R CARDINGTON GLANCED at the clock on the wall and realised he should have left the office a good twenty minutes ago. His fellow bridge players would be kept waiting, doubtless drumming their fingers and making jokes at his expense. He capped his fountain pen and sighed. He would have to stand them all an extra round of drinks for his tardiness. The papers on his desk still needed to be filed away properly, too.

'Can't leave confidential legal papers all over the place for the cleaners to peer at,' he joked to himself, wincing slightly at how the previously comforting silence was disturbed by his voice. He glanced up at his open door and through into the reception room where his assistant worked and greeted clients. Of course, young Stanley Cribbs had said his evening farewells almost an hour earlier so the ante-room was quiet and still, illuminated by just a couple of wall lamps. His eyes seemed to be held entranced by the view through the door frame, as if there was something there, just out of sight.

He could see, to the left of his portrait-framed view, the edge of Stanley's desk; a segment of oval rug lurking behind it in the centre of the floor; while to the right of this lifeless still life, bookshelves pressed along the wall. Peeking out at the top and bottom were the curving bare limbs of a hat and coat stand.

Cardington realised he had been holding his breath and let it out. His throat felt dry. He really needed a drink down at the club. Or two. But mostly he needed to get out of the office.

He gathered his paperwork together and tapped it hurriedly into square order before sliding the loose pages into a manila folder. He had just clipped the folder closed when he heard a sound from the ante-room: the brief but alarmingly loud bray of a wooden chair leg moving a few inches on the wooden floor.

Cardington's heart had almost leapt from his throat and was now pounding away like a steam train, his ears echoing with thudding pulses. He tried to swallow but his mouth was like a desert, no moisture and, other than a faint whispering of breath, no sound. He eventually mustered enough control to call out loudly, if not terribly confidently, 'Hello? Who's there?'

An almost silent static hiss of fabric in motion reached his ears, but no-one answered him.

'Hello? S-Stanley?' he asked again.

And now he could tell that feet were moving across the floor of the room beyond. He stared through the doorway at the still motionless slice of room, fingers gripped tightly around his forgotten folder.

His eyes widened as a shapeless shadow entered the frame, moving slowly from the left, onto the rug and turning towards the door. The lights in the room struggled to throw any definition onto the shape but he felt that he was looking at a woman, dressed in black, possibly with some form of headwear. He could discern no face, the shadows and perhaps a veil preventing any hope of identification. A second shadowy figure now stood at her side. A man by the look of him, thought Cardington as he reined in his alarm and began to wonder who they were and what they could possibly want at this time in the evening.

'Sorry, can I help you?' he said, rising out of his chair.

The figures stopped just beyond the threshold to his office. The lamp on his desk completely failed to help him make out any more detail of his visitors. The woman took a step into his office and spoke with a dull, muffled voice. 'Mr Cardington?'

'Yes,' he replied, 'I'm Mr Cardington, owner of this practice.'

The man now followed the woman into the room. 'We know,' he said.

'Well, my name is on the door I suppose...' he began.

'No,' interrupted the woman, 'we... know, Mr Cardington. About Captain Sykes.'

The solicitor blinked and paused before responding. 'About... the *late* Captain Sykes? Ship lost at sea, what, three years ago? 1919 was it?'

He looked at them expectantly. 'And?'

'And Mrs Sykes,' said the shadowy man.

'Ah, yes, so that would also be, ah, the *late* Mrs Sykes. Terribly unfortunate, so soon after hearing the news of her husband. So, how can I help you?'

'And,' continued the woman ignoring him, 'their children.'

Mr Cardington looked at them and frowned. 'I'm sorry, who are you? I'm afraid I can't discuss confidential legal affairs with just anyone, you know.'

The couple took another step closer to his desk. An unusual mix of aromas percolated into the air around them. Sea weed and oil; lilies and damp earth.

'There is a trust fund,' said the man with a voice that sounded as if it came from far away. 'For the children. That you drew up. That you now draw *on*.'

'A-ha,' laughed the lawyer, nervously, 'yes, well, it's still there. Yes, I am the trustee and have some *limited* access, for investment purposes and what have you. Rest assured, once the children turn twenty one they will gain access to a fine inheritance.'

The woman seemed to tremble as she leant forward and said, 'The children need it now. You must release the funds to my...' she paused, 'to their aunt.'

'I'm sorry, but the fund was set up to pass an inheritance on to the children of the late Captain Sykes once they become adults. And, when Mrs Sykes passed away, *her* estate also went into the trust.' He looked from one shadowy figure to the other. 'If only the late Mrs Sykes had signed her estate over to her sister in the event of her death...'

The woman took another almost shambling step forward and held out a crumpled document. The lawyer cautiously reached out, took it from her black-gloved fingers and examined it.

'This appears to be the last will of the late Mrs Sykes, but...' he frowned once more as he turned the pages, 'but it's the version she never signed.'

'It is signed,' said the woman, raising her hands to her black veil.

'Signed?' muttered Cardington, looking incredulously at the signature on the bottom, 'but how?'

The woman lifted her veil, drawing his eyes up to the macabre horror of her face. 'Better *late* than never,' she whispered.

DANCING FLAME

by Peter Graves

"*LADIES AND GENTLEMEN!* The Golden Globe is proud to introduce FLAME the most exotic dancer on the West Midlands circuit! Tonight is her final appearance before she begins a world tour to delight international audiences with the charms that we saw first here at the Golden Globe."

The slightly faded red velvet curtains remained tantalisingly closed as the music, Ravel's *Bolero* burst forth from the large speakers on either side of the room. The curtains opened to reveal an empty stage with the statutory bent wood chair, painted in patchy gold with an obviously wonky leg.

Flame appeared and the whole room was filled with excitement. The men looking up at the stage, mostly British Leyland workers from nearby Longbridge, lusted after her. She was fantasy incarnate. From the mass of golden hair framing her fabulous face and tumbling in sensuous waves over her shoulders she was special. Her figure was something you did not see every day, even in the glamour magazines of which most of the men in the audience were connoisseurs. Her elegantly manicured finger nails and toe nails were part of the dream before them, matching perfectly the fiery gold of her flame coloured hair.

The women in the audience adopted quite a different attitude. As one, they tried to imagine how she, this Flame, this creature of totally unreal fantasy, would cope with the demands of the everyday life. She would not cope like proper women with cooking, cleaning and a couple of kids whimpering for attention all the time.

With an aloof expression and appearing not even to see what was going on around her, the delectable Flame moved erotically, discarding piece by trivial piece of her flimsy costume and dropping them disdainfully on the bentwood chair.

Eventually, totally naked, she received the tumultuous cheers from the men in the room and, not noticing the silence of the women, left the stage. She made her way to the pokey little cupboard called a dressing room. All the trappings of voluptuous glamour were packed into her cheap holdall, the wig, the nail extensions and the pouch of cosmetics. She counted all the bits of her so-called dress and packed them together into a Tesco bag. Dressed in her cheap jumper, jeans and anorak she took her thick spectacles from her handbag and slipped them on, breathing a sigh of relief that the world was sharp-edged again.

Arriving at the front door of her first floor flat, she found her key and struggled as usual to get it into the lock. As she pushed into the hallway, past the pram and the little two wheeled bike, she reflected on the women who were scattered among the audience at the club tonight. She could not help but wonder how they would cope with the demands of her life. Could they really manage to do the cooking, cleaning, a couple of kids whimpering for attention all day *and* still be able to look like a dream in the evening? She picked up a letter that was lying on the doormat. Hopefully this was confirmation of her new council house near her parents in Walsall. She glanced at the front before she opened it just to make sure it was for her and indeed it was; her name typed neatly at the top - Miss Janet Bunsen.

TRENTSIDE

by Peter Day

Pale and tired
the woman's refuge
on the quiet river bank
is near the field
where flax ripples
as a length of blue satin
(her favourite colour);
the waves drift
as calm undulating sleep.
The warm southern wind
scented by ripe beans
washes the river bank;
the fragrant air is for her
more beautiful than sorrow.
After two boats sail from the marina
she sees no one;
she hesitates,
then walks down river.

A raven calls from the high ash tree;
she shudders,
recalling its ominous reputation.

Apprehensive now
she fears ghosts
rushing with the weir's torrent.
The pale body
is seen, though half concealed,
on the quiet river bank
a week later.

SWIFTLY WE MUST GO

by Anne Howkins

*T*HE SUDDEN MOMENT *when you realise that it's time to move on again seems to happen more frequently. And it's that time again, the end of summer, I feel the need to fly south with the songbirds.*

I wake slowly, as white light creeps under heavy eyelids, catching the scream of the swifts as they tear their way down the street, out-squawking the alarm. I wriggle around for a while, chasing the comfort that effervesces just as I think it's firmly in my grasp.

Showering slowly, I let hot water wash-rinse away the ghosts of last night's reverie. Fresh livid purple flowers over fading yellow on my thighs and forearms, tender to the lightest touch. Muscles scream their protest as I tentatively stretch under the soothing heat, breathing steam to relieve the tightness in my chest. She'd gone too far this time, we can't carry on like this.

Wrapped in soft towels, I write a message on the steam frosted mirror. 'We need to talk. I can't take any more.' And sign it with our name.

Gingerly I dress for work as the coffee machine does its stuff — I need the caffeine hit to jump start this shattered body. Before her festering anger erupted we would breakfast together, wiping flaky croissants from each other's mouths as the screeching swifts chased insects below us. Covering fragile limbs with opaque cloth, to hide my shame from prying eyes, is an effort. The slightest movement sucks the breath away from me. This time she's marked my face. Another line in the sand crossed. I wince as I dab concealer over the damage. Finally a spray of scent and I'm ready to face the world and all that the day will bring. As I close the door I glance back to the inert mass amongst crumpled bed-linen, knowing she's not going to like what she hears tonight.

I love the familiar walk to work, feel my body loosening as I dodge the kids on the way to school. The office is at full throttle as I arrive, some rush job creating the buzz we thrive on. I ease myself into my chair, hoping to avoid attention, trying not to look at the two familiar photos pinned up on the wall. A blue eyed brunette smiling for the camera, bikini-clad on the beach and partying in a night club — everyone thinks it's me in both of them.

A cup of coffee appears in front of me. I turn my head to meet Dave's smirk.

'You were well up for it last night,' he said 'we couldn't keep up with you. Again. How the fuck do you do this, out all hours, what's the secret?'

'If only you knew.'

'Take something when you go home to feed the cat?' he sniggers. For months he's been teasing me about going home after work before we all go out. I think they've all fallen for the single girl alone with a cat malarkey.

'Well, work your magic on this one.' He dumps a file on my desk and saunters off, whistling some pop melody about a brown-eyed girl that will stick in my head all day.

I bury myself in the mess of paperwork, doing what I do best, bringing order to chaos. Dave's tuneless notes keep disturbing me, bringing my thoughts back to her. I try to feel what she is doing right now, hoping it's something safe. I know she can't go out, but I can't stop unexpected visitors being enticed into the flat. My phone trills, almost the same notes as Dave's irritating pop song. I check the screen to see who wants to talk.

'Hi Meg' I start tentatively, aware that she may have been party to last night's events.

'Hey Josie, you at work?'

'Yup, got a big job to sort through.'

'How do you do it? Last night...'

I interrupt her 'Yes I know, not sure, I don't need a lot of sleep.'

'Just wanted to make sure you were OK. That bloke you were talking to when we all left, he turned up in A & E this morning. Head wound, covered in bruises and what looks like bite marks. Won't say what happened, he's in a state though. Any ideas?'

Meg spends her days patching people up, coping with everything society throws at her. She's my closest friend. Sometimes I almost tell her my story, now I'm glad I haven't.

'Oh god. He was fine when I left him, just after you all went.' The lie came easily. 'Are the police involved?'

'No, he refuses to speak to them. Won't say how he got hurt, says he got into a fight with a mate, but I'm not sure. But if he won't say, I can't do anything. Just hope there isn't someone out there hurt.'

'Well not me, I hope he's OK. Sorry Meg, got to dash, I'm buried.'

Motion seizes me, makes my legs move. Fighting nausea, I leave my desk, I must get into the open air. We've reached the nadir of our hell-like existence, time to make some changes, get her back under control. I don't know how much longer I can keep doing this, nothing stops the cycle.

Dave is outside, puffing away on the edge of the smoker's vile enclave.

'Josie, what's up? Seen a ghost?'

'Meg's just told me...that bloke last night...he's been beaten up or something...in a bad way.'

He throws his fag away and puts an arm round my shoulder.

'You're shaking. Thought you'd only just met him.'

'Yes, I had, it's just the shock. Poor guy. I want to go and see him. See if I can help.'

A knowing smile spreads over Dave's broad face. I decide to let him think his lascivious thoughts.

'I'll tell the boss, say you've had some bad news. Off you toddle then...'

The flat is deadly quiet as I let myself in; even the swifts are silent after giving up their chase in the midday sun. My legs give way as I close the door behind me, sending me sprawled against the wall. Now the pain starts, each bruise yelling for relief. I want to wash it all away with tears, feel hot salt cleansing my skin. I feel her presence, a gentle touch on my shoulder. Her vague form wavers in front of me, swaying with the motes dancing in sunlight streaming through dirty windows. I can't look, close my eyes waiting for her to cleave this damaged body in two. Take away at least half the pain.

We sit facing each other, fingertips touching, eyes closed, breathing together, building the energy for what is to come.

'You've gone too far...' her thumb presses my lips together. This time I summon the strength to brush her touch away. 'What happened last night?'

Her eyes widen, and a faint smile appears on her pale face. She slowly traces the outline of a bruise on my arm and avoids my questioning eyes.

The energy in her touch changes. I move my arm as her probing fingers find pain. She is shaping her own body, pulling energy from me and from her dreadful deeds. She holds her arm out, flexes long pale digits as two pairs of eyes watch in silence. She wants me to yield, let her take over, so she can go out, she wants the daylight, not just the dark. I'm scared at just how far she might go. That other line in the sand she's almost crossed. I feel myself shrinking, my hands are becoming translucent. I must stop her.

A gust of wind sends curtains billowing, startling the resting swifts. Piercing cries vibrate through the flat, spurring us out of our trance.

'I have to go and see him.'

I force myself up, away from her, out of the door before she knows I'm going. Her screeching follows me as I stumble out onto the pavement. Dark shapes wheel away from the building as her shouts startle the agitated birds again.

Somehow, I get to the hospital. While my nerve holds, I go to A & E and ask the receptionist to tell Meg I need to see her urgently.

As Meg appears, she looks at me and shakes her head. Leads me to an empty curtained off cubicle, sits me down.

'Cardiac arrest, a few minutes ago. He's in intensive care...'

Terror washes over me, slides me to the floor again. Somehow Meg is holding me, easing me back into the chair, calming the earthquake inside. She calls a nurse, talks of shock, gives instructions about my care; gently tells me she has to get back to her patients; that she will return as quickly as she can.

Like a newborn I allow the nurse to manipulate damaged arms out of my jacket. Her badge says she's called Sarah. She doesn't notice that I see her face tighten at the bruises; that I hear the 'tut' she allows to escape under her breath. She gently washes the tears and streaked make-up from my stony mask. Then her probing fingers find damage on my cheekbone.

'That's a nasty bruise on your face. Who hurt you?'

Sarah doesn't know the real reason I'm here. She talks of X-rays, says she'll get Meg back to look at me. I nod, then she's gone. I slip off the bed, grab my things and get out before anyone can stop me.

As I retrace my steps, the air is heavy with the threat of thunder, sending the swifts into a frenzy of feeding, building their strength before the long flight to winter warmth. A police car flashes past me, stops outside the block of flats where she is raging against my absence. I slip into my local coffee shop.

'Hey Josie, are you OK? Here, let me get you an espresso, sit down.'

I shrug at Brian's kindness, follow his instructions. He puts a cup in front of me, with a flaky croissant, my usual weekend treat, and then looks through the window.

'There's some hoo-ha at your block. What's going on?'

Two blue figures emerge, holding a struggling form, dark hair flying as her head swivels in a swirling rage. Her shrieks fill the street.

Poor Brian, he doesn't deserve hot coffee down his pristine apron. I apologise and mop at him with inadequate paper napkins. He disappears behind the counter as I watch her being driven away. A pale face stares at me from the back window. Her spleen rattles inside my taut head as the car rounds the corner.

Freshly draped, Brian reappears with more coffee and sits down with me. Slowly I raise my eyes to meet his as he takes my hand.

'Josie, something's not right. Is that girl your sister? I always wondered if you lived with someone else. The person I see going out isn't you. It's not just the make up and the clothes...'

I shake my head and tell him that I am going away for a while. Some family business abroad that draws me southward. I tell him I will call back in a few minutes to pay for my coffee.

'No worries pet, on the house. You look after yourself, come back safe.' He kisses my forehead so tenderly I can't help the slow trickle of salt running down my ashen trembling cheeks.

The flat door is ajar. I peep in, see that she's trashed the place. A few weeks ago she was too weak to move without my body. She has fed on her nightly violence — but she will soon fade. I wonder how long it will be before her fragile form needs me again.

Throwing a few clothes into my backpack, I dig out passport and emergency cash and cards from under the floorboards. I move quickly, fearing they will be back to search the flat properly.

As I go back out to the street and head for the station, the swifts are on the wing. Sleek dark shapes, careering without a care, always on the move.

'Bye-bye birdies, I'll be waiting for you.'

GUARDIAN ANGEL

by Brenda Millhouse

H E'S HAD ENOUGH of nothing to live for any more. There was no point in locking the door, he wouldn't be going back. It was raining, but it suited his mood perfectly. He was nearly there, walking along the river bank, looking for a suitable spot, when it happened. One minute he was the only person in the world and the next he had collided with a tall man wearing a dark coat and wide brimmed hat. His bowed head looked up into the most piercing blue eyes he had ever seen in his life.

'Would you be kind enough to buy a raffle ticket?' the stranger asked.

Some strange force compelled him to dip his hand into the pocket of his jacket for change. He couldn't escape from the steadfast, almost compassionate gaze that held his eyes as he asked 'What's the prize?'

The voice that answered was soft but clear, gentle, but with an almost hypnotic commanding tone. 'It's a mystery prize, but of great value'. He wanted to be on his own again.

'How much do you want?'

The stranger smiled, his face seeming to radiate light in the previously dark night. 'What ever you think they are worth'.

He looked at the coins in his hand. What did it matter? He wouldn't be needing money. £1.75 seemed a small price to pay for the solitude he desired. He handed it over in exchange for a crisp piece of paper.

'Thank you. I'm sure you won't regret it'.

Just GO he thought, but he didn't. Ending one's life is a private thing, spectators are not an option, so muttering a resentful 'Good night' he turned and headed for home. He could feel the penetrating gaze even with his back turned. An invisible power controlling his unwilling legs, making them backtrack his steps completely. Back inside the house he angrily pulled the ticket from the pocket it had been thrust into and examined it. It was completely blank.

The doorbell rang. Wasn't he to be allowed any peace? He walked back along the uninviting hallway and jerked open the door. Standing there was a man, well a clothed body; he couldn't make out a face.

It spoke, the ethereal voice seeming to percolate from the whole being, not just the invisible mouth. 'I've brought the prize you won in the raffle'.

An almost translucent hand emerged from the depths of dark folds and held out a small sealed envelope. As he reached out and accepted it he could feel a hard object inside. He opened his mouth in automatic thanks but no sound would come, for no one was there to hear it. The hand that closed the door was, like the rest of his body, now icy cold and shaking. There was nothing else in the envelope, just the key. Not gold, not silver, a strange combination of the two. The suicidal thoughts were replaced by curiosity. You need a concentrated but empty mind for that, and his was full of tall strangers, mysterious raffles and unusual keys. There was always tomorrow. He couldn't help but think that it was a long time since he had thought that. The idea of tomorrow had been miserably unacceptable for so long. The decision made again, he went to bed actually looking forward to this one.

He was awoken by the doorbell. Stumbling, still half asleep, down the stairs he opened the door with relief to a very normal looking postman. 'Sorry mate, but you need to sign for this'.

He took the offered biro and scribbled his name in the appropriate spot on the form held out for him in exchange for a brown paper parcel. He removed the wrapping to reveal a green metal box. It was locked. The key was on the sideboard where he'd left it last night. He picked it up and tried it in the keyhole. As he turned it easily and was about to lift the lid, he felt himself being drawn inward, sucked into a vacuum, the intense blue bright light was blinding, then pitch black darkness. He tentatively stretched out his arm and felt cold metal. Turning instinctively towards a faint crackling noise, he found himself looking at a TV set. The picture flickered, then cleared to reveal a broad brimmed hat, dark coat, and those unforgettable vivid eyes.

Mesmerised, he stared at the screen. The voice was still comfortably soothing. 'My name is Martin, and I'm your Guardian Angel'. Answering the question before it was asked, he continued. 'We don't wear our wings all the time you know, would you prefer it if I changed?' The incredulous shake of the head was noted. 'The ticket you bought last night was Life itself, but the prize was something more important. The key to wanting to be Alive.' The picture flickered once again, then disappeared. Another image appeared, one he recognised immediately — himself. The surroundings were unfamiliar though. A summer time beach, crowded with holidaymakers, but not unbearably so. He was walking across firm golden sand towards the tempting sea hand in hand with a small girl. The unseen camera zoomed in on a close up of an adorably pretty five year old, her almost white blonde hair held back in a pony tail, staring up at his face.

'Is it really easy to swim Daddy?' she asked with the unquestioning trust that children of that age bestow on their parents.

'Yes of course it is darling' he heard himself reply.

'Then I'm going to do it then. You won't let me sink will you? I love you Daddy'.

A child, this child, even a part of her would be enough reason. The tears that flowed in the obscurity of darkness were easily detected by Martin. 'I hope I've given you the will to want life, but to keep it you need to fight. It's yours if you fight hard enough'. The TV screen went blank.

He wanted it, more desperately than he thought it possible to desire anything. The metal box like room suddenly became a prison that he had to escape from and not the airless coffin that he had wished himself into. A tiny chink of light above him caught his eye. The keyhole. He's unlocked the box; if he could open the lid he could be free. Feeling his way across to the far corner of the room, he tore the TV set from its socket, and half carried, half dragged until it was beneath the beckoning brightness. He then climbed up onto the top of the makeshift step and found he could just manage to reach the ceiling. He reached up and pushed. It yielded to his efforts, and a long horizontal slit of light appeared. Making a desperate leap, he managed to grab hold of the hard edge and wedge his head and shoulders in the gap. The weight forced the air from his lungs, but gasping for every breath he finally succeeded in hauling himself out. He could see the floor of his living room below. Shutting his eyes he let himself drop.

The innocuous box sat on the sideboard with a key in the lock. He sat in a chair, thinking of a daughter who had yet to be born, and looking forward to the future.

DISCOVERY

by Diane McClymont

THE ROAR OF the bulldozer had stopped half an hour ago. Frank had been watching the activity in the back field from his kitchen window.

He knew why the work had stopped. He knew this would happen. This was the reason for his protests against the development of the land for new houses.

The locals had been very surprised by his outrage. 'Usually such a quiet man,' he heard them whispering. 'Poor old Frank; lives all alone. His wife upped and left him many years ago; just disappeared. The new houses will certainly spoil his view.'

They would spoil more than that, he thought.

He watched as the police arrived and cordoned off an area. They'd soon work it all out.

No-one would understand, He sat down at the table, picked up the glass and began to swallow the tablets.

INTERVIEW WITH A KILLER

by Jackie Leitch

WHERE DO YOU want me to start? With Joe? I'm not really sure I want to talk about that... OK, then, let's get it over. Yes, I deliberately killed him. Now I suppose you want to know why. Simple. It was him or me. I'd grown to hate him. I was afraid; afraid he would be the death of me. So, I got in first. That's one answer. Another is that I needed him. I knew that one day it would all come to an end; he would have to go and I was afraid of coping without him. So, I killed him quick to get it over and done with. Want a third? OK. Something between the two. I both needed and hated him. I was afraid of his violence and what it meant to be part of it. I wanted to be free of him yet was scared of being without him. Who would give my life meaning and purpose if he wasn't in it? I was a wreck with him and shambles without him. So, I killed him out of ... what? A desire to end the confusion? A need to be free? A longing to have the inevitable over and done with? You decide. At the time, I decided it was necessary. What more do you want me to say? I killed him – that's an end to it.

It had begun very differently; with hope and trepidation. A relationship balanced on the edge of great success or miserable failure. Joe James was my creature, my creation. I write detective fiction and he was my best and best-loved character. I poured my heart and soul into creating him. But gradually he took over my life. He started off a bit of a rogue; a good-looking, quick-tempered, opera-loving Private Eye who dispensed justice to career criminals throughout seven books. Joe had an ex-wife, a gambling problem and some dodgy friends. The readers loved him. I topped the best-selling author charts with five out of the seven novels. Success, eh? At a cost, though. Over the series, Joe became increasingly short-fused. The justice he meted out became rougher and more lawless as he resorted to vicious beatings to solve the crimes he was investigating. The murders themselves became more gruesome and repulsive and Joe's wild violence and barely contained fury took us closer and closer to the edge with each novel. The violence became an end in itself. The fans loved it, couldn't get enough. Me? I was worried. His character was getting away from me and starting to live a life I had not planned. He was writing himself as a brutal maverick who took the idea of an eye for an eye to its logical conclusion.

Even the process of writing seemed out of my control. Most of the time, I hardly knew what was happening. The mornings are my most productive time but by book five I was writing all day, forgetting to eat and drink. Writing book six was like living in an hallucination. Whole days would pass and I'd barely surface at all. I became exhausted and prone to fits of rage. I trashed my living room in the early hours once because I couldn't find a specific CD. Opera as it happened. Number six broke all the records for sales. The critics lavished it with praise. The Guardian said *'the brutal nihilism and darkness at the heart of the novel resonates with the moral emptiness of modern society'*. That's as may be but I hadn't intended any of it and the novel didn't seem like mine.

I put off starting book seven for a long time. Eventually I was driven to it because the ideas and dialogue running in a loop in my brain were driving me half-mad. Also, my agent was pestering me for the next novel. I decided then to rid myself of Joe and his malign influence. So, I can say with all honesty that I killed him. Joe died heroically, as he would have wanted, but it was a horrifyingly cruel death, as I wanted.

When he read what I'd done, my agent was furious. My publisher wasn't very happy either. We were all making a good deal of money out of Joe James and they didn't see any reason for this to stop. They badgered and bullied me to rewrite the ending but I was adamant. It was him or me. In the end, we didn't do too badly out of Joe's demise. We sold the film rights for "One Last Time" to Quentin Tarantino's people. It's right up his street. Perhaps John Travolta will play Joe.

So, my next novel? Yeah, it's coming on well and I'm really pleased with it so far. It's set in the 1870s and features an ex-cavalry officer who gets caught up in a murder on the London to Edinburgh train. I'm not making the same mistake with Major Brookes as I did with Joe. No more loveable rascals for me. After the trauma of killing off Joe, I needed a different direction. So, Major Arthur Dante Brookes is a model of probity and right-thinking. Hopefully, he won't get out of hand. If he does, I'll kill him too.

THE NEEDLE

by Joan Stephenson

MISS DOROTHY PILKINGTON looked round her very own drawing room. The wall paper, the paint, the furniture all of her own choosing. She had waited sixty years for these things and, much as she had loved her mother, she had never felt anything but cramped all her life till now.

She moved her shoulders a little, a gesture she used so often nowadays, rather like a stretching of wings.

She switched off the television set (a new experience, that) turned on an extra lamp and took up a piece of sewing, lying rather untidily beside her on the sofa.

Bother! Needles had become harder to thread lately. In spite of her ninety years her mother had been an expert needle threader, expert at everything, really.

Dorothy tried all the old tricks, holding the white thread against her black dress; moistening the end with saliva and twisting it round to a stiff point; in desperation even moistening the eye of the needle. It was almost as if her mother were back in the room, telling her, as she always had, what to do next.

She sighed and gave it up as a bad job, did those bed-time tasks her mother had always insisted upon; unplugged the television set, checked both doors back and front that had been locked and checked over three hours before. Then with another little twitch of the shoulders she deliberately left out the clock winding and went to bed.

She slept well, as she always did. Next morning she opened her eyes to the light and wallowed in the promise of another whole day to herself.

No quavering, 'Good morning, Dorothy,' to answer; no running of somebody else's bath, always too hot or too cold; no other egg to boil but her own, always too hard or too soft; no splitting of the daily paper and, best of all, no waiting to get at the crossword.

About ten o'clock, in her own good time, she started to tidy the drawing room. Not much to do, really, other than fold up the piece of needlework that had so defeated her the night before. Bother again! Where was that wretched needle? Dangerous thing, needles, to be left lying about in upholstery. She shook each cushion, even getting down on her hands and knees to search the carpet. All without success.

It wasn't until six that evening when she switched on the news that her eye caught a glint on the little wine table, the only piece of furniture left that had once belonged to her mother. And there it was, the needle, double threaded with a knot in the end that had always irritated her. Her own preference was to secure with a back stitch.

Her shoulders' twitch turned into a sag. She looked down at the table and up to the ceiling.

'Thank you, Mother,' she was about to say. Instead she braced herself and glared at the wine table.

'You're for the sale room tomorrow, my lad.'

HUSH

by Linda Cooper

MARCIE'S EYES FLICKED open but the darkness rendered it impossible to work out where she was. Exposed limbs and the cold wall behind her aching back forced her to acknowledge it definitely wasn't at home in bed. The stillness of the air confirmed she was not outside but a penetrating chill added force to the tremors she was having difficulty controlling. Not a flicker of light from any direction convinced her she must be in a basement, attic, cellar or a room with no windows. Either that or she was blind. The disjointed jigsaw pieces of her brain struggled to recall how she came to be here, wherever it was, but no flashbacks or memories could fight their way through the swirling mass of confusion. A tight, sick feeling lifted into her mouth as she tried to swallow the metallic taste of fear. She had no idea whether it was day or night; even if her wristwatch had been on her arm she still wouldn't have known. But she could have put it to her ear, listened to it ticking; the deathly quiet was unnerving her more than the darkness. Marcie had never felt comfortable with silence.

Even in a safe environment the sound of the wind, birdsong, the familiar hum of the refrigerator were not enough; her first automatic action of the day to turn on the radio; drown silence with friendly voices and distracting music. Here, the silence roared; Marcie wanted to fill it with loud screaming but her voice was paralysed by the same terror that pinned her motionless to the wall. The only thing she could hear was the manic rhythm of the pulse in her ears. She must move.

Crawling, Marcie inched forward over the cold, stone floor, recoiling as her fingers brushed over something warm and sticky. A small part of her felt grateful the darkness prevented her from seeing what it might be, but her ears would have welcomed even the sound of a rat scampering over the floor rather than this unearthly silence. Every second that passed carried the weight of a century of dread. Finally, her hands discovered steps, but the tiny glimmer of hope evaporated like morning dew as a heavy wooden door opened and a flood of light illuminated a silhouette. Marcie's memory returned; she wished it hadn't.

The corners and sides of the jigsaw fell into place but as yet she couldn't see the whole picture. Shielding her eyes from the sudden glare, she rose to face the woman she had not known existed until yesterday.

'Please,' she begged, her voice barely a whisper, 'Can we talk about this?'

'Shut it,' was the only reply she received. 'Make one sound and there'll be much worse than this in store. Understand?' The door slammed shut as swiftly as it had opened, plunging Marcie back into darkness. Muffled conversation between a male and female faded away leaving Marcie alone once more with her thoughts, her anger and the deafening silence. She recognised the man's voice but knew now he was not the man she'd believed him to be. If she could only turn back time twenty-four hours; a year would be even better.

Almost twelve months ago Marcie met Ben at a party and thought at long last she'd found the man of her dreams.

Generous, charming and attentive with an air of mystery that kept Marcie interested Ben had swept her off her feet almost instantly. Their relationship blossomed and intensified, convincing Marcie her future was secure. But then a few weeks ago she'd discovered she was pregnant. Ben's reaction had disappointed and shocked her.

'You have to get rid of it,' he'd stated firmly. 'I'll fix you an appointment as soon as possible.'

'But Ben...'

'No buts Marcie. I'm not ready to be saddled with kids yet and I don't want anything spoiling our relationship.' Marcie had sensed desperation behind his calm, measured reasoning but also a distinct feeling that should she not comply, she may never see him again. And that was one thought she couldn't handle.

Reluctantly she agreed; within days Ben escorted her to a private clinic, paying the bill for a termination. Kissing her tearful, frightened face before leaving he promised he'd be in touch once she was home.

The abortion affected Marcie more severely than she could ever have imagined. Emotionally, she wasn't coping; waking each morning to dark thoughts, bitter resentment and a deep longing for her lost baby. Nights of disturbed fitful sleep left her exhausted and weepy; not wanting to face the day ahead. As time dragged by and there was still no word from Ben, her disturbed mental state deteriorated. The heartache for the baby she now longed to hear crying for the first time and the constant nagging voices in her head could be obliterated by the radio no longer. Then, last Monday she'd received a letter.

'Darling Marcie,

I need to see you. Please come to the above address at three 'o clock on Wednesday. There's something I want to show you.

All my love, Ben.'

Although angered by his lack of concern for her ordeal, she was relieved to hear from him at last; optimistic they could pick up the pieces and everything would be fine.

But when she arrived at the address, it wasn't Ben who answered the door but an unfamiliar, enraged woman who obviously knew of Marcie. It didn't need the brain of Britain to work out it wasn't Ben who'd written the letter but his wife, whose existence Marcie had never suspected. Shocked and stunned, she was given no time to offer an explanation.

'Bitch,' the woman spat. 'Husbands aren't safe with women like you around.'

Marcie opened her mouth to defend herself but before she could utter a word she was hauled into the house and none too gently pushed down the steps into the windowless, silent room she was now confined in. She could try screaming, make Ben aware of her presence but no longer had any idea how he'd react or what lengths his scorned wife would go to. Sweating and shaking, adrenalin pumping like a mountain spring Marcie brought her trembling knees to her chin, rocking rhythmically. Fear paralysed her to the spot; traumatised eyes gazed blankly into the still pitch of the room and in the eerie silence she had no control over her rampaging mind.

An eternity seemed to pass in the black void before the door opened once more. Marcie's vacant expression barely altered as the figure descended the stairs brandishing a glistening carving knife.

'Get up.' The hissing wife yanked Marcie on to her unsteady feet before prodding her forwards up the steps with the point of the blade piercing her back. Once out of the gloom, malicious eyes bored into Marcie's expressionless face.

'You've been warned,' the voice continued, the knife hovering dangerously close to Marcie's throat. 'Go anywhere near Ben and I'll make sure you never see or hear anything again.

Now get out.' Blinding sunlight assaulted Marcie as she was propelled at speed through the front door, but not before she'd heard a familiar noise from the bedroom at the top of the deeply carpeted stairs; a sound that tightened still further every muscle in her body and forced her empty womb to contract painfully.

Her captor, satisfied her vicious threats would send Marcie running like a gazelle pursued by a hungry lion failed to notice the shadowy figure creeping around to the rear of the house or the click of the back door as a deranged Marcie tiptoed past the lounge and ascended the stairs.

'Hush,' she whispered to the gurgling occupant of the wooden cot as she placed a pillow firmly over its face. If Ben preferred to be childless Marcie was perfectly willing to oblige.

Never before had the sound of silence felt so deeply satisfying.

KING RICHARD III RIDES AGAIN

By N.K. Rowe

RICHARD III, THE last Plantagenet king of England, opened his eyes and immediately winced. There was a dull light glowing softly around him but he couldn't make out any other details. He realised he was lying on his back, staring at a distant dark ceiling. This was odd. He decided to try sitting up.

'Ow, my head!' he cried out, as pain danced around his upright noggin, 'I feel like I've been hit with a pole-axe!'

'Funnily enough, you were', a voice said from the other side of the room or chamber or where-ever Richard was now sitting. He swung his head towards the voice, trying to make out a blurry figure.

'Who are you?' he demanded. Richard wasn't sure if it was his eyes or a trick of the light, but the blurry figure was becoming more solid. And there were two others with him.

The first figure, a man in fine clothes, stepped forward. 'We are your spirit guardians and companions, Sire. We served you in life and watch over you in death', he said with a bow.

Richard, rubbing his temples to ease his headache, squinted at the shortest of the three figures. 'I recognise you! You bring me my breakfast. Any chance of a spot of porridge? I'm starving. I'm sure I can feel my ribs.'

The young woman curtsied politely but looked uncomfortably embarrassed as she replied, 'Alas.... no'.

'No? Hmm.' Richard wasn't used to being refused. He was a King after all.

The third ghost now stepped forward, some kind of royal page by the look of him thought Richard. 'The pole-axe your Highness mentioned...'

'Yes...?'

'...knocked the life clean out of you.'

The King stared at the three figures. 'What do you mean?' he asked, suddenly becoming aware that he was still sat on some kind of low bench or table. He stood up, trying to make sense of where he was and how he got here. 'The last thing I remember was... a battle'. Brief memories of swords and lances and horses and mud and terrible fighting skipped around his head.

'Yes Sire, over at Bosworth against Henry Tudor', said the man in lordly clothing, who Richard was sure was one of his advisors in York.

Bosworth! Henry Tudor! Those names clanged heavily with Richard, like keys to a prison cell of memory. 'Yes, that's right!' he exclaimed, 'a battle against that scurvy knave!' But the memory, released with enthusiasm from the cell ran face first into more locked doors. Richard couldn't remember how the battle had ended. 'Erm, how did I do?' he asked his attendants.

They looked awkward, shuffling and fidgeting and not meeting his eye. The breakfast maid, unable to think of a better way to break the news eventually blurted out 'We'll give you three guesses'.

The other two looked at her with irritation before the first figure said gravely, 'I'm sorry, my Lord, all was lost'. Then all three clasped their hands together and bowed their heads.

'Oh,' said Richard, feeling as if he had been punched. 'And Henry?'

'He became King Henry the Seventh,' said the page, 'and started the House of Tudor, my Lord.'

If Richard felt like he had been punched before, this felt as though someone had just kicked him in the crown jewels. 'Damn and blast!' he shouted, 'Not just a Lancastrian King but a Welsh one too!' He paced angrily around the chamber, fuming. 'Well,' he added, 'I hope he gets his come-uppance!'

'His unfortunate family,' began the advisor from York, 'was full of sorry tales of woe. Tales which have been taught to schoolchildren for hundreds of years'.

'Good!' said the King, stopping his angry stomping with a smirk. Then he frowned. Something was still not at all right. His memory abruptly stopped thinking about battles and picked over what he had been told since he woke up. He felt a bit faint and swallowed dryly. 'Erm... You said 'hundreds of years'?'

'Yes, Sire' replied the advisor.

Richard looked down at his gloved hand. He could clearly see the tiles on the floor through what should have been an inch or so of fine leather, skin, flesh and bone. Oh dear, he thought.

'How long...' he began, before swallowing again and taking a deep breath, 'how long have I been asleep? I mean...'

'Dead, Sire?' said the advisor, 'Five hundred and thirty years.'

Richard rocked backwards very slightly. Good grief, he thought, that's a very long time. 'And the Tudors have gone?'

'Yes, after them the Crown went to James,' said the page. 'A Scot'.

'Ye gods!' exclaimed the King, 'first a Welshman and now a Scot! You'll be telling me next that all of Europe are taking turns with my kingdom!'

'Well,' continued the page with just a smidge too much informality, 'there's been a Dutchman and a few Germans, as well as a stint when they got rid of kings altogether.' He caught the eye of the fuming royal and lowered his head, 'Shocking business, Sire. It ain't been the same since you've been gone.'

'So tell me', said Richard icily, 'who is King of England now?'

'Elizabeth, Sire,' said the maid.

Richard blinked. 'That's a funny name for a King.'

The advisor coughed politely, 'Elizabeth the Second is Queen, my Lord.'

Richard blinked again. 'A QUEEN?!?! Whoever heard of such nonsense? And the second one, eh? Who was the first?'

'Elizabeth the First was Henry Tudor's grand-daughter,' explained the advisor.

'I might have known!' said Richard, flinging his arms in the air. 'Those Tudors can't even make a decent male heir to the throne!' He walked around the chamber shaking his head and tutting. A thought struck him and stopped. 'But what of *my* place in history?' He turned to his spirit servants and raised an eyebrow. 'Do the people know about their dear old King Richard?'

'Which one?' said the page, 'They're quite keen on the Lionheart.'

'Me, you fool!' shouted the irate monarch, 'Richard the Third! Come on, tell me, how do people remember me?'

'Well,' began the maid, 'there was this amazing playwright called William Shakespeare...' Before she could continue the advisor from York had pulled her and the page over to the far corner away from the King.

'You can't tell him about the Shakespeare play!' he whispered angrily, 'He'll get upset!'

The maid glared at him, 'He'll find out about it eventually though.'

'Well, let's leave that for later, not now,' said the advisor, 'I think he's a little delicate at the moment.'

'Yes,' agreed the page, 'finding out that people think you're an evil hunch-backed murderer does tend to spoil your day.'

'What was that?' said Richard from behind them.

'Nothing!' said the startled spooks, guiltily.

'Hmmm,' said the King, gazing at each in turn. 'So you were telling me how the people remember me.'

'Well, Sire,' said the advisor, 'you are definitely one of the more well-known kings.'

'Especially now', agreed the maid.

'Especially now,' repeated Richard. 'Yes, now about that... I am some kind of... ghost... am I not?'

'Yes, Sire,' agreed the advisor, 'well done, Sire.'

'But why now? Why has it taken over five hundred years....'

'To get your spirit up, Sire?' asked the page.

'Yes. I'm not sure how all this works, but it does seem a very long time.'

The advisor from York stepped forward once more. 'There have been some, ah, 'developments' with your burial place. Your original tomb was in Greyfriars in Leicester...'

'But,' the page chipped in, 'Henry Tudor's son got into a bit of an argument with the Pope and the friary was demolished...'

Richard shook his head in disbelief, 'Those cursed Tudors again!'

'....and your tomb was lost for hundreds of years,' finished the page.

'Until you were found under a car park,' said the maid.

'Under a what?' asked the King, puzzled.

'A car park.'

'Is that good?'

'Well,' continued the maid, 'finding a space in a car park is often challenging, finding a King is amazing!'

'So,' said the page, 'you were dug up and examined.'

'Examined?!?' Richard suddenly felt uncomfortably exposed and brought his arms in to cover his body.

'Yes, to make sure you were you, Sire,' said the page with a grin.

'And you are,' said the advisor reassuringly, 'congratulations, Sire!'

Richard, still with his arms across his torso, tried to make sense of it all. 'Well, that explains why I feel so... 'bony'.' He looked around the chamber, noticing for the first time that it wasn't entirely enclosed. Detail beyond a few yards was lost in a kind of dark fog, but he got the impression that they were in a large building. 'So, where am I now?'

The advisor waved his hand and the fog began to clear, 'You've been entombed in Leicester Cathedral...'

'With a big fancy ceremony!' said the maid.

'...and everyone came to pay their respects,' continued the advisor.

'Even Sherlock Holmes,' said the page, 'it was a lovely service.'

Richard, watching as more and more of the ancient cathedral seemed to congeal into view, noticed a group of strangely dressed people approaching. The one in front pointed directly at the dead monarch.

'And here we have the tomb of King Richard,' said the guide, passing right through the King and gesturing at the big ivory-coloured bench on which Richard had been lying. Richard now realised that it wasn't a bench at all, but his tombstone. It was long and low and cut with a deep cross from edge to edge. He nodded his head in approval at the size and majesty of the stone, although it seemed a little spartan. In his day a proper tombstone had a full-size statue of the deceased carved on top.

'Wow,' said one of the group, 'Is he inside that?'

'No,' replied the guide, 'He is buried under it.'

The thought of his actual body trapped under such a weighty stone made Richard feel distinctly uneasy.

Another of the group piped up: 'That's a big chunk of stone. Is it to make sure they don't lose him again?'

Richard stepped over to his attendants. 'Who the blazes are they?'

'Tourists,' said the advisor, 'come to see your tomb.'

'You mean pilgrims, come to pay their respects to their dear old king?'

'Well...' began the maid.

'Sort of...' said the page.

One of the group was nudging another. 'Go on,' she said, 'do the famous line.'

'Oh alright,' replied her friend, before theatrically exclaiming: 'A horse! A horse! My kingdom for a horse!'

The King turned to the advisor. 'Why did she say that?'

'Oh, they're supposed to be some of your last words, Sire.'

'Are they?' Richard furrowed his brow in concentration. More images of his final battle drifted through his memory. 'I really don't remember saying that. As I recall... it was more like 'Oww, argghhh!! Gettoff!!'' The King nodded to himself slightly, 'But you know, I think I prefer that horse one.'

The tourists were now beginning to drift off, following the guide to another part of the cathedral. A small child was left staring at the tomb with folded arms and dark expression. Her mother called to her to come along at which point the child turned and said grumpily, 'But what about the skellington? I want to see the skellington!'

The child stomped back to her mother, obviously unimpressed that the day's most interesting item was hidden under a mass of stone. As Richard watched her go, wondering whether the girl would be quite so forthright and stroppy after a few nights in the Tower, his attendants came before him and bowed.

'And now, Sire,' said the advisor from York, 'we will leave you to your slumbers.'

'My slumbers?' said the King, confused, 'Not likely! I've been dead to the world for five hundred and thirty years!' He saw sunlight twinkling through the stained glass windows and more unusually attired people walking down the aisle. His mind was made up. 'I'm off sight-seeing!'

'But Sire...' said the advisor anxiously, pointing to the tomb, 'your final resting place!'

'Yes, yes, good to know the old bones are finally being well looked after,' said the King rubbing his hands together, 'but I need a ride, some phantom nag to carry me.' A thought struck him. 'Let's see: A horse, a horse, my... erm...' he patted at his ghostly garments and extracted a fine handkerchief. 'My hankie for a horse!'

From the dim recesses of the Cathedral and the darkened edges of reality came the sound of a ghostly neigh and ironclad hooves. King Richard III smiled. 'Splendid!' he said as he strode off to mount his spectral beast and explore this new world.

His attendants stood, unseen, uncertain and unwanted.

'We waited five hundred and thirty years for that,' said the advisor from York. 'What do we do now?'

The page turned to the maid. 'It's a lovely summer's day,' he said, holding out his arm, 'fancy an ice cream?'

'Don't mind if I do,' she replied, taking his arm.

'But what about the King?' hissed the advisor.

'He can get his own,' said the page.

ON THE WAY TO O'NEIL'S

By Sean Gaughan

A CLEAR, STARRY NIGHT; a slender moon illuminating little but the vague outline of the crooked road Colm Mullarkey (father of the potato-headed Mick Mullarkey and a good many other louts) and his friend Joseph Murphy, a slow-witted naive kind of man, were taking towards Glenowen and Jonjo O'Neil's public house. Mullarkey lobbed a desultory cobble at an inoffensive donkey hanging its head over a gate and, a couple of fields later, the same again at a Kerry cow quietly chewing the cud. It's not easy to see a black cow in the dark but Mullarkey had the eyes of an owl and the hearing to match. He could detect the tinkle of a sixpenny piece falling from a pedestrian's pocket and veer across the road to scoop it up and into his own without breaking his stride, so his cobble easily found its mark, sending the docile creature thundering into the darkness, bellowing angrily.

But sure, there was little else to entertain anyone travelling a country lane at that time of night. And there would be little happening at O'Neil's pub for the next couple of hours at least, until the lame fiddler from Blacksod got a few pints inside of him and struck up a tune. Then Breda O'Bryan might start up doing a bit of a shimmy and showing her legs, providing her father Ned was in the other bar and she well out of his sight. And then someone would say what a slut she was becoming and she'd hear him and throw a glass of beer at him and some young buck would jump to her defence, hoping for favours later, and then some kind of a set-to would ensue and a table might go over and O'Neil would raise hell about his broken glasses and send for the Gard Dan Doyle in the next house down the road. Sergeant Doyle was a great one for the rough-house. He'd wade into the thick of it laying about him in all directions at once, cracking heads and breaking noses with his baton. But when it was all over he'd return home and resume whatever he'd been doing as if nothing had happened; he'd never dream of summoning a man to court and, in the morning, would pass the time of day with last night's adversaries as if they were old friends. Which they probably were.

Another reason why Jonjo O'Neil welcomed Gard Doyle into the pub was because he was not a man to interfere with free trade. He never passed comment on the hours O'Neil kept, not even when he served customers until seven in the morning.

As Mullarkey and Murphy rounded the bend before the hill into Glenowen they could just about discern the fallen rocks that strewed the road.

'They say there's the face of Saint Patrick up on that cliff,' said Joe Murphy.

'There is, right enough,' replied Colm Mullarkey. 'My lad Mick seen it and he pointed it out to the priest.'

'And what did Father Nolan make of it?'

'He told Mick he was a feckin' heathen eejit.'

'He didn't say 'fecking' did he?' asked the mildly spoken Murphy.

'Well, maybe he didn't. But that's what he meant to say. And anyway, it's Nolan who's the eejit. If he'd a brain in his head he'd have it broadcast in the newspapers and then we'd soon have a shrine in our midst like at Knock, or Croagh Patrick, and we'd all have money made out of the pilgrims. And then,' continued the enterprising Mullarkey with a grand sweeping gesture, 'there's that big shallow rock-pool on the other side of the road. We could have all the cripples in the land dipped into it and them leaping out like hares, all cured of their afflictions. It might have made this the richest place in Ireland.'

'Sure, there's no depth to that pool, is there?' said Murphy, peering into the gloom. 'Ye can only poke a stick into it a few inches before ye'r into thick mud.'

'It's deeper than you'd think. I've seen it empty and cleaned out.'

'Ye'r a great man, Colm; I'm always amazed at what ye know. How did that come about?'

'Can ye remember around twenty-odd years ago, there was a farmer named Hennessey lived the other side of the mountain; had a wife named Annie-Kate?'

'I do remember,' said Murphy, 'they were both great drinkers.'

'That they were, and the drink was the cause of the pool being emptied.'

'How was that?'

Mullarkey paused and surveyed the road, picturing a night from twenty years past and pointed in the direction they were heading. 'They were returning from O'Neil's pub one night and she'd too much drink taken...'

'She must have had a fair drop taken indeed,' interrupted Murphy, 'she'd the stomach of an ox on her and could drink stout as fast as the brewery could produce it.'

'She could, but this particular night it got the better of her and she puked into the pool and lost both her spectacles and the set of false teeth Hennessey had had made for her.'

'And they emptied the pool to find some specs and false teeth?' said Murphy, dubiously.

'Well, Hennessey had paid big money for the teeth and wanted them found.'

'Aye, they've too much money, these farmers.'

'They have.'

Murphy turned his back on the pool that glistened like black treacle under the moon. 'But why did he spend so much? I didn't know he thought that much of her.'

'He didn't. In fact, he belted her in the gob for losing the teeth.'

Murphy nodded with wise insight. 'I suppose that was his opportunity, her mouth being empty. He'd hardly want to risk breaking them when they were in place. But what was so special about them? Could he not just get her another set made?'

Mullarkey, revelling in the authoritative role of narrator, raised a finger to indicate the crucial point. 'She wanted them to look more like natural teeth so asked him to have gold fillings put it. She had a mouth like a bucket and it must have looked worse when it was all gum and tongue, so ye can't blame Hennessey for going along with it. What's more, he thought the gold would be a sound long-term investment should he ever fall on hard times.'

Murphy said nothing, pondering how gold made teeth look more natural. He was fairly sure that he didn't have any gold in his mouth. Or perhaps he did. He'd look in the mirror in the morning. It seemed a reasonable explanation for why anyone would want to become a dentist. It was probably a bit like prospecting.

'The next day,' continued Mullarkey, enjoying the sound of his own voice telling the tale, 'Hennessey paid a few bob to three school kids to have them empty out the pool. So two of 'em climbed in, mud and water up over their waists to begin with, and spent the next two days bucketing and shovelling the muck over the side and away down the hill. They'd stationed the third lad a bit down the hill with a rake and he pulled the dross apart as they threw it towards him.'

'Did they find the teeth?'

'They did,' said Mullarkey, 'but not in the pool. They'd fallen in the heather close to the road, along with the spectacles. But of course, without the spectacles she was as blind as a bat, and in any case they were both dead drunk at the time and wouldn't have found their own arses with both hands. One of the lads came across the specs by standing on them. The glass had broken and fallen out but he put them on, thought they gave him the appearance of an intellectual. He wore them for years afterwards. He thought he was James feckin' Joyce. And then they found the teeth at their feet. Hennessey gave Annie-Kate another quick belt before she got them back into her mouth for causing him to have to pay the lads for emptying that feckin' pool which was, would ye believe, about twice the size of my pig-sty and three or four feet deep. It's the shape of a scallop shell, which is ideal. If a pilgrim were standing in it taking a cure he'd have the holy face of Saint Patrick looking at him from across the road with the hills behind, and a view in the other direction across the heather to the sea. The view alone could make ye feel better, even if it didn't cure ye.'

A long silence lingered around them as Murphy contemplated the problems of turning the place into a holy shrine supporting local commerce. His brow furrowed. 'How would the people taking the water avoid exposing themselves getting in and out of the pool?' He was not a man to countenance any glimpse of nudity.

'It could be managed,' said Mullarkey, 'they could put fences around it somehow. A problem easily resolved if only

Nolan would apply himself to it. But that's the main problem, of course. The man has no business head on him.'

Murphy was giving further consideration to the idea of fleecing pilgrims. 'But what if they were not cured?' he asked.

'That's made no difference at Lourdes,' replied Mullarkey, 'that place has been thriving for years.'

'But,' persisted Murphy, 'some of 'em do get cured there. Like Edna McCarthy. Before she took the waters there she walked like a hobbled cow. Now she swings her hips wonderfully and walks all over the place like there's no tomorrow.'

'They say she had legs of different lengths before she went to Lourdes. One was said to be two inches longer than the other.'

'Sure, that would account for the way she walked,' said Murphy as he dwelt upon this for a full minute. 'Who do ye think measured them?'

'I dunno,' said Mullarkey, still focused on pilgrims rather than Edna's pins. There was another long pause whilst Murphy's brain ticked over.

'It wouldn't have been McNally, would it?' he eventually asked.

'McNally? The schoolmaster? Why would he have a ruler up her skirt?'

'I just thought it might be him. They do say he's very precise with figures. If I was getting my legs measured I'd want someone like him to do it.'

The pair spent a couple of minutes looking at one side of the road and then the other, pondering the mercantile potential of the place, silent except for the tapping and scraping of their feet. Murphy began nodding. 'Ye'r right Colm. It's a pity they deported Father Tom to Cork. He'd have made something of it.'

'Sure, Tom McGrath was a different man altogether,' enjoined Mullarkey with enthusiastic fondness in his memory of the priest. 'He had his head screwed on all right. He could change a penny-piece into a pound note any day of the week.'

'It was a great shame indeed that they moved him. I suppose he didn't do himself any favours importing that big black Studebaker from the States. Even with his financial miracle working it must have stretched the parish funds a bit.'

'If only he'd succeeded in convincing the bishop that he was buying it as a hearse for the benefit of the parish so they didn't have to bring the dead to church by horse and cart, he might just have got away with it. I'm sure the shorter coffins slid onto the back seats with no bother. But the bishop was another one with no head for business.' Mullarkey shook his head at the error of men's ways.

Murphy was still mulling over the erstwhile Father Tom and his legendary abilities, both pecuniary and spiritual. 'I wish we had Father Tom back here to cure the pilgrims. They say that he was good at curing women's infertility.'

'He did seem to have that about him,' agreed Mullarkey. 'A good many women conceived after asking for his help.'

'And yet they sent him away,' sighed Murphy.

'Ah, sure the old ones were hard to beat,' said Mullarkey, kicking a stone and shoving his hands in his pockets. With one last glance at the rock face of Saint Patrick they ambled up the hill towards O'Neil's.

Extract from the forthcoming novel "Artistic Licence"

THE BLACK DRESS

by Val Woolley

MARY LIKED TO plan things. First she would make notes randomly on the back of an envelope, then she would group together various ideas, circling them in red biro, and finally she would make her list. Using a sheet of pale blue Basildon Bond notepaper, and her black pen, she would write out the 'to do' items. It gave her great deal of satisfaction to make a neat tick against the item, on completion. When they were first married Bryan used to laugh at her for her lists.

'It doesn't really matter if you forget something,' he would say, and Mary would shake her head and insist that to her it did matter. Bryan found Mary's lists both exasperating and helpful. When they were going on holiday everything would be washed, and neatly packed. Nothing was ever forgotten, but should he suggest an impromptu picnic, or a trip to the seaside, Mary would simply refuse to go, giving him silly excuses like 'My coat's at the cleaners,' or 'we don't have a thermos flask'.

Bryan got used to it over the years, but he did find that his life was rather dull and boring, and then he met Lola. He was working late, one evening, and she just walked into his office, and into his life. Just like that. Dressed in the tightest pair of jeans and a tight tee shirt, showing the ample curve of her bust, she teetered around the office in high heels.

'Shall I just empty your waste bin, and come back later?' Lola asked.

Bryan stared at her, 'No, don't go.' he told her, and Lola stayed, and life for Bryan became exciting at last. If Mary noticed the change in her husband she said nothing, and their life together went on as usual. Feeling slightly guilty about Lola, Bryan tentatively suggested that perhaps instead of their usual two weeks in Eastbourne, they should have a week in Paris instead. He was astounded when Mary agreed, but true to his word he booked a trip to Paris. As he expected Mary immediately began to make lists.

'I shall need a new dress' she told Bryan, and added much to his surprise, 'I want you to come and help me choose it.' Bryan was astounded, he had been shopping with Lola, waiting while she tried on the skimpy tops and the tight jeans she was so fond of, but he had never, in all his married life, been dress shopping with Mary. Bryan took a half day's holiday, and they went into town together. He had expected Mary to want to go to Marks and Spencer's, or even Debenhams, but instead Mary chose a small exclusive boutique just off the Exchange Walk.

'Black,' Mary told the proprietor, 'very chic and very classy. We are going to Paris you know.' The woman hid a smile, and produced a beautiful cocktail dress in midnight blue. Bryan thought it suited his wife very well, but Mary frowned her disapproval, although she did try it on. She stared at her reflection in the mirror.

'It looks lovely dear,' said Bryan.

'Do you have the same in black?' she asked the proprietor. The lady shook her head, 'But I do have a different black dress in your size. It is one of those dresses that you can wear for anything.' Mary tried the black dress on. It was, as the woman said, very stylish, but it didn't suit her as well as the blue one.

'Why not have both?' Bryan suggested, knowing that Lola would not have been seen dead in the black dress.

'No, I came in for a black dress, it's on my list.'

Bryan mentally shrugged his shoulders, and paid the bill.

'Now how about afternoon tea at the Royal' he suggested, and again much to his surprise Mary agreed. They had thin cut sandwiches, scones and two pots of Earl Grey. Bryan found himself actually enjoying his wife's company; perhaps a week with her in Paris would not be so bad after all. They walked slowly back to the car park, Mary carrying the new dress in its very smart dress box. While Bryan paid for their parking, Mary walked round to the front of the car, and looked down over the car park wall. Eight floors below, the traffic was building up.

'Just look at this,' she called, as Bryan unlocked the car. 'I can't believe what I'm seeing.'

Bryan walked to the wall and stood next to her.

'Down there to your left.' Mary shifted the dress box to her other hand.

Bryan twisted round to peer over the wall; it was then that the dress box caught him on the shoulder. He knew he was falling and he held his hand out to Mary as though expecting her to catch hold of him. She was already phoning for an ambulance.

After that everything became a blur. People crowding around; blue flashing lights, and then the echoing sound of footsteps in the hospital waiting room. A man in a suit came out of the office and walked towards her. Mary knew what he was going to say. She opened her handbag and took out her list. On the pale blue paper there were only two items, she ticked 'Buy Black Dress' and then circled the other one, the one that read 'Arrange Funeral'.

SARDINES

by Anne Howkins

THIS TIME THERE'S no excuse not to go back. I haven't been to the village since I was ten and spent Easter holidays with Aunt Helen there. That was before my stroppy phase when nobody wanted my company.

It's a lovely house in a great area — it'll get me a nice chunk of commission. I'll clear off the credit cards, maybe even get a holiday. Going to be tricky though. The vendor's son died in an accident twenty years ago. Her husband jumped off a Tube platform the year after. She'd called the agency, asking for me to handle the sale. I was flattered, and for once the blokes didn't object. I don't remember a child dying. Maybe Helen told me, but I didn't listen to anyone then. I'm still like that sometimes. There's a switch in my head that just trips when things get too much.

So here I am ringing the doorbell, wondering why my stomach is on a spin cycle and my foot is tapping out Morse code. Mrs Cooper invites me in. She spins her wheelchair away and I follow her into a sunny sitting room, all squashy sofas, polished mahogany and antique vases stuffed with gorgeous flowers.

'I'll show you round the house Chloe, you'll have to do the grounds yourself. You understand why?'

I nod assent, my voice has disappeared. I pull out my notebook, ignoring my usual recorder. As I measure and make notes Mrs Cooper seems oblivious to my growing unease, her attention directed at a silver charm bracelet her fingers work silently. Normally I'd be chatty, gleaning information to pass to prospective purchasers, but here it seems wrong. It will be a relief to leave her in the house and explore the garden.

As I step onto the stone terrace, she tells me she needs to rest, and that I should leave when I have finished in the garden. I hear the key turn in the French window lock, and she is gone. My foot is tapping again. Oh, stop it I tell myself you're just worried about her, that's all, you've done the worst bit.

I step onto the manicured lawn and the world spins...

'Right kids.' Mr Cooper's voice booms out, silencing the chatter. 'Sardines? Who's going to hide? Isn't it Chloe's turn?'

A babble of voices shouts him down.

'She doesn't know where.'

'Nah, she's always gives up.'

'Not sissy Chloe.'

They scare me, these hideous boys with their cruel taunts and sharp poking fingers. I shrink back towards Mr Cooper as James darts off through the shrubbery.

'One hundred, ninety-nine...' Six breaking voices chant the ritual countdown while I shrink inside myself.

And then, a starburst of lithe bodies explodes over the lawn, leaving me shivering in its wake.

'Go on Chloe, show those lads what you're made of.'

Mr Cooper takes his G&T back to grownups relieved of their parental chores.

James was right, I always give up. Humiliation is the safer option. The first time I went to the house I joined in, eager to be seen as one of the boys. How stupid I was. Aunt Helen had chosen to believe that I'd torn and bloodied my pants climbing a tree. In those days nobody questioned injured little girls too closely. The boys always ended up filthy with ripped clothes after an afternoon in James Cooper's garden. Why would I be any different?

I shuffle about in the shrubbery for a while. I can hear whoops from the orchard.

'Chloe, Chloeeee.'

James is taunting, daring me to find them.

I know where they are. Then something really stupid flashes through my head. If they're in the shed I can shut them in. Make them beg to be let out. I tread carefully, keeping off the gravel path, stopping every few feet to listen to their noise. After an age, I reach the run-down outhouse.

No, please no. The door is half off its hinges, pulled as wide as it can open. I flatten myself against the wall and hold my breath. They mustn't hear me.

'Silly cunt. She can't find us.'

Oliver mutters something and the others hoot. Someone says something about gin. Then there's a thud. Their voices fade, drowned by the cloudburst that is soaking me.

I creep around the side, and carefully peek through the cob-webbed window, sucking my lip to stop my teeth chattering.

There's a huge freezer in the middle of the floor, but no sign of the boys. The lid is down. I peer through the dirty glass. There's lots of thumping and muffled voices coming from the chest. I stare for what seems like hours, willing it to stay closed. I realise that I am dribbling and scrub at my mouth. My hand comes away red. I've bitten my lip.

And then I notice the catch on the lid. I'm safe.

'I hate you stupid boys.' I yell and yell at the rusty old box until my throat is hoarse. When I stop everything is quiet. A warm flood soaks my trousers. Blood still drips down my chin. I want mum.

Helen rushes over to me as I appear at the French windows and hushes my sobs. She whisks me to a bathroom, gently undresses me and swaddles me in a warm fluffy bathrobe. Mrs Cooper asks where the boys are. Helen speaks sharply, something about the boys being unkind, and then we are home.

'I'm sorry' she whispers as she tucks me into bed, 'I didn't realise how horrid the boys were to you. I won't take you there again.' A little while later the screech of sirens and the ghost of a blue light flashes across the ceiling as I drift to sleep.

'There's blood on your hands.' Mrs Cooper passes me a tissue. I'm sitting on the stone steps, warm scarlet dripping through fingers wrapped round my face, trying to hold back years of not knowing as it seeps through my skin.

INSIGHT, OUT OF MIND

by Brenda Millhouse

SHE HESITATED SLIGHTLY before she pushed open the door. Ten minutes had elapsed since she'd stepped from the transporter which had dropped her off on the opposite side of the broadway. She was early, and her appointment wasn't until ten o clock. The time had been spent viewing the shop from a safe distance. A large neon sign was flashing intermittently in shades of purple and red, KNOW YOUR OWN MIND.

It was too late to change hers now, it was made up. After all, everyone was doing it these days. Brain implants were as common as face lifts and breast enhancement had been way back in the 90's and early 2000's. She could remember being told about those days, as a small child. A vision of her ever youthful looking mother filled her mind. It was all so easy now, just a daily pill or a monthly painless injection of serum and you could stay looking whatever age you chose to. Pensioners had to carry their birth papers around with them if they wanted to avail themselves of the benefits available to those over 150 years old.

She'd thought that she and Bradley would be in love for ever, after all they had signed the Together Pact and exchanged the plutonium tokens which had replaced the old fashioned marriage ceremony. After ten years together though they had ended up living on different planets - quite literally. She needed him out of her head - and her mind.

She stood in front of the huge tower in the centre of the shop, as it slowly turned, allowing her eyes access to the choice. Hanging on hooks around the tower were sealed clear packets containing what looked like small lumps of transparent jelly. All in alphabetical order, they dangled invitingly before her. Adventurous and Arrogant right through to Zany. She was allowed to choose fifteen according to the instructions displayed on the wall. She took her time and chose carefully, after all this was to be the new her. She had to get it right, she hadn't been given the choice with her first one, her parents had decided what she would be.

Soft modern music played as the white coated assistant led her to the mind clearing room. It was filled with iridescent blue light, which somehow managed to calm her thoughts. In an almost hypnotic state she lay on the low couch provided and without being asked put on the pair of heavy chrome headphones which had been sitting on the metal table next to it.

The assistant quickly tightened the clamp then flicked a switch, and for a few moments the pressure was unbearably painful. Then she felt nothing. As though in the distance she saw a tornado like spiral of her life disappear. She was oblivious to being wheeled into the adjoining room The technician was waiting with her choice laid in an orderly row in front of him. Syringe after syringe was filled and accurately fired at high speed through her skull into each waiting vacant space. Finally a last dose of anti-rejection fluid, and it was done. She opened her eyes and lay still for a few seconds. She didn't *feel* any different. Perhaps it needed a while to take effect.

'The transfer went very well, you may leave whenever you feel in control. Payment is by cash or earnings transfer. My assistant will see to the details'. The robotic technician had already switched his attention to the jar of brain cells extracted earlier, and was separating them out to be packaged and recycled on the tower.

The assistant readily accepted her cash payment of 2000 Zecrons, not much plastic money was circulating at the moment, and it made it so much more simple for him to supplement the meagre wage he was paid. He entered a discount of 25% on the clinic records, pocketed the difference, and went into the inner room to collect the freshly sealed and labelled sachets. As he hung them on the appropriate hooks of the tower, he gradually became more and more surprised. For Articulate, Brave, Caring, Cheerful, Considerate, Fascinating, Generous, Humorous, Independent, Imaginative, Intelligent, Kind, Loving, Sensitive, and Witty filled the empty spaces exactly.

THE AZALEAS

by Diane McClymont

THE '*AZALEAS FOR sale*' notice was nailed outside the fence, uneven letters painted in tar on a piece of board which he had found in the shed. He'd put it up this morning secretly hoping no-one would want to buy them. He wasn't even sure how much to charge for them: they were priceless to him. Several years he had spent cross-pollinating , patiently waiting for the results, trying something new — yes, they were indeed a labour of love. *She* had said they were an obsession: that he spent more time with his rotten plants in that damn greenhouse than he did with her. Well, that was true.

Since his retirement he had been at a loose end: never knew what to do. Indoors he always seemed to be in Mary's way. She was for ever cleaning and polishing and he, apparently, made the place look untidy. He'd got used to keeping out of the way on Tuesdays when a group of ladies met to discuss books or poetry or whatever and alternate Thursdays he was quite happy to disappear when Mary's sister called. She was a first class snob and no mistake.

So to keep himself busy he'd developed his love of Azaleas. They were beautiful plants with masses of colourful flowers in late April, May time. Their garden was a picture and often admired and Mary seemed quite happy about that.

But then about five years ago he had got talking to an expert at a flower show who was proudly showing off a new variety. He had been fascinated and after reading many books on the subject began his own experiments. It wasn't easy and required patience and dedication which seemed to puzzle Mary. He had to admit that she was right when she said that they hadn't had a holiday for ages because he couldn't trust anyone else to water and look after his plants. Oh yes, everything she had said yesterday evening was correct. She had really gone wild; ranted and raved for a good half hour about their marriage, their lives etc. and finally delivered the ultimatum, 'Either those blasted Azaleas go or I do! It's up to you George.'

Well, he liked a quiet life and Mary had been a good wife in many ways and was an excellent cook so what choice had he got?

He had got up early this morning and dug up the azaleas in the garden and potted up the smaller ones for sale. He had destroyed all his experimental ones. No chance of fame now. Later on he was going into town to book a holiday in Spain for the pair of them. He hoped that would soften the blow when Mary discovered that he had ordered several tons of concrete to cover their garden. If he couldn't grow Azaleas then, he was very sorry, but he wouldn't grow anything.

DREAMING OF STARS

by Jackie Leitch

THE SAND IS both soft and hard; soft in my fingers as I run them through the grains, hard beneath my body. I lie straight, my arms outstretched. It's about 4 a.m. and I am very drunk.

There are no street lamps in this small, remote coastal town in Western Australia, therefore no light pollution. Just a rich blue-black sky alive with brilliant starlight and the perfect sphere of the moon casting soft pale shadows. Tentatively, I open my eyes again. This time, the stars and moon do not dance around like whirling dervishes. *Maybe I'm sobering up,* I think. I have never seen so many stars before: the Southern Hemisphere has far more stars than the cold grey-black night sky in my Northern European home. The sheer beauty – and possibly the alcohol – bring tears to my eyes. The still figure beside me stirs. I thought he was sleeping but, no, he too is awake and enjoying the lightshow. Neither of us speak, the moment is too precious for words. He takes my hand in his and loosely links our fingers. We could be alone in the world; the absence of sound or streetlights or people confers a kind of freedom to be no more than we are at that moment, two

159

human-beings, side by side on the shore of a land more ancient than any other.

Donny gives a faint grunt as he untangles our fingers and sits up. 'Sleepy. Gotta go to bed.' he mumbles. Planting a soft kiss on my cheek he stands up, momentarily blocking out the moon. Staggering slightly, he leaves me alone in the night. I do not reply or acknowledge him in any way, too caught up in the shimmer and glitter of the night and the whoosh of alcohol through my blood. Perhaps tonight I will sleep without terror invading my dreams.

At last, even I tire of the beauty. I have looked for so long that the spectacle has become commonplace. The wooden cabin we are staying in is only a short stumble from the beach. Donny is deep in sleep as I strip off my shorts and T-shirt and fall into bed. At first, I find it hard to drift off, the bed seems unstable, liable to veer one way or the other; a few times I find myself clutching at the edge of the mattress, fearful that I might fall out. When, finally, sleep overcomes me, it is disturbed by jumbled dreams and fearful encounters. Awaking fitfully, the hot little cabin feels claustrophobic and sweaty, the air pressing in on me. Irritated, I throw off the tangled covers and slide away into dreams again.

Donny has gone for his usual swim by the time I wake up. I straighten the bed-covers and pick up a lone feather from the floor. *Only two more days here at Coral Bay*, I think, *then it's time to move on*. Without thinking, I push the feather into the pocket of my shorts then start to make a simple breakfast of fruit, pancakes and coffee. Glancing at my watch, I wonder where Donny has got to. *Lost track of the time*, I tell myself, *nothing to worry about*. Minutes pass, then half an hour more has gone. I go to the door. The German couple from two cabins down are walking back from the beach, hand in hand.

GOBSTOPPERS, SHRIMPS AND SOUR MONKEYS

'Hi', I call, 'Did you see Donny around?' I try not to sound over-anxious.

'No, Grace.' Axel replies and Kristin shakes her head too. 'We are all alone on the beach. No-one else is there.'

I try to sound casual, as if it was just a passing comment. 'OK, thanks.'

They step up onto the decking and come over to the door.

'Are you worrying, Grace?' Kristin asks, with a frown of concern.

Axel puts a hand each side of the door-frame and leans in, the sunshine highlighting the red-gold of his stubble.

'You need some help maybe?' he offers.

Obviously, I had not sounded as casual as I had thought.

'No, not really.' I deny. Then my fear spills out, panicky words stumbling one over another. 'Only, y'know, he doesn't usually swim for longer than half an hour, and... and he was already gone when I woke up more than an hour ago.'

My voice sounds strange to me, more sob than speech, choked and yet shrill. By now, I am making no attempt to sound unconcerned. Putting my worries into words has made them more real. I can feel myself verging on hysteria, my heart pounds and my legs go weak and shaky. The dread is real. Now, here, in the daytime. Kristin puts out her hand, runs it gently along my arm, 'Come then, Grace, we will look together for Donny.' Axel nods his agreement. The three of us walk back to the beach in the hot, still air.

The small office out of which the lone policeman operates is blessedly air-conditioned. Even so, I can feel myself sweating with apprehension. He writes down everything I tell him in my anxious, wobbly voice. He asks questions I cannot answer. 'So, do you have any idea what time he went off for his swim?', and, 'Did he always go at the same time?', and, 'You say you didn't hear him go?' and many more until my story begins to sound odd and disjointed, and I feel disconnected from the events of the morning, as if it is happening to someone else. The questions are unbearable to me, I wish he would just stop questioning everything I say and go look for Donny.

Axel and Kristin take their turn to tell the policeman what they know. They have little to add to my story. After all, they only came onto the scene after Donny had already gone. They are keen to be helpful, and give Germanically precise answers but they really have nothing to say. The Sergeant is kind, 'Don't worry Ms Jackson, we'll take a gander round, he's probably gone off for some more bread or beer and forgotten how long he's been gone.'

I try to smile but my heart is beating so hard in my throat, I cannot concentrate on making my muscles form a smile, not even a small one.

I stop off to see Ray, owner of the half-a-dozen cabins on the site. I explain what happened; the visit to the police and my fears for Donny. He is sympathetic but unconcerned. Putting an arm round my shoulders, he tries to reassure me. 'No worries, sweetheart. Stay as long as you like. I'll bet ya Donny'll be back before ya know it. And Mac's a decent bloke, he'll see ya right. Anyway, it's quiet around here for now, just you, Axel and Kristin, so I enjoy having you kids about. You're quite an ornament around the place.'

His voice booms in my head. My frown of pain seems to mean something else to him. He grimaces and pats my shoulder as if the thought had just struck him that his comment might sound somehow inappropriate. 'Who's Mac?' I think, then realise it is Sergeant Campbell.

The cabin provides no form of respite from the ugly thoughts running through my mind. So many questions. Later, the Sergeant comes to find me again. I must go to the station to give a formal statement and sign it. The atmosphere in the small office is less relaxed and more unreal even than before. Axel and Kristin have been asked to return, too. They go in after me. I cannot hear what is being said as Sergeant Campbell has closed the door this time. It seems to me that they are in there for quite a long time. When they come out, though, they are much the same as usual with me. Their manner is gentle and concerned; their behaviour is kindly and they do not seem anxious or strange in my company. Somehow, this comes as a relief.

The Sergeant drops us off at the cabins, saying he wants a word with Ray anyway, so it is no problem to give us a lift. *What kind of a word does he want with Ray?* I wonder. Answering my own question, I realise he will want to ask about Donny and I, how we seem together; see if there had been any raised voices, arguments? Anything to suggest we are not the loving couple we appear to be at first sight.

The following day the Sergeant comes for me again. I am to be questioned further about what I remember.

'Just to get everything clear in our own minds.' the Sergeant explains.

It seemed to me that it was perfectly clear the first time I said it, I thought. We go over it all again; he asks, I answer. I feel close to tears. 'What more can I say?' I ask him, 'I've told you everything I know.'

Disturbed nights and exhaustion take their toll. My dreams are troubling, horrifying, most nights filled with bewildering images. Not only am I grief stricken, to add to my woes I feel I am becoming paranoid. Axel and Kristin try to be positive, supportive; their kindness gets on my nerves after a while. What I want is to be left alone, no more questions, no more 'talking it over', whatever that means. What I need is Donny back with me, loving me, calming me. Sometimes, my fear turns to anger.

I stalk about the cabin, muttering out loud, telling Donny how furious I am with him for just going off like that. What was he thinking, leaving me alone and vulnerable in a strange country? In my mind, I shout at him, give him a good telling off, make him understand how frightened he has made me. It does not last, the anger, I go down to the shore and walk along the waterline, crying and pleading with Donny to return to me.

Donny is nowhere to be found. Belatedly, the police Sergeant searches our cabin, going carefully through Donny's things; rifling through the paperback he was reading - a second-hand copy of Dan Brown's 'Da Vinci Code' bought in our local Oxfam. He takes his time feeling through Donny's clothes; then examines the bed and bedding. He takes everything out of Donny's wallet; the credit cards, some receipts, his driving licence, scraps of paper with 'phone numbers and email addresses on, his U.K. driving licence. There is nothing of any significance, nothing to cause a man to disappear. Now, the Sergeant turns his attention to our travel documents, our suitcases, my clothes. We do not have much with us, so he is soon done with our belongings. He opens the cupboards, drawers, looks at the knives.

'Were there any tools in the cabin?'

I give a small shrug and shake my head, not sure what he is after.

'You know, wrenches or spanners, screwdrivers, that sort of thing? Maybe a shovel?'

'No.' I say.

Next, he searches our hired car, pulls out the spare tire, examines the jack. Later, he returns with two more men. They poke and prod with long poles along the seashore above the high-water mark, pushing the poles into the dense sand and then into the soft thin soil the cabin stands on. When they are done, he tells me to stay in Coral Bay for now.

'Until we see where we are ...' He trails off, appearing uncomfortable and ill-at ease with what he has to say.

I know where I am, I think, *I'm in Coral Bay without Donny.* I wonder where the Sergeant is going with his thinking. Despite the heat, I feel chilled.

'Do you think I killed him?' I ask, my voice squeaky and shaky. I sound guilty even to myself.

'No, it's just procedure, Ms Jackson. Just routine.' he assures me. I am not convinced. I know he thinks that Donny is dead and I am responsible.

The police check hospitals all along the coast, few and far between though they are. They put out alerts and call on the public for any sightings. They issue a description: 'White male, 5'7' tall, small boned and of slim build. Aged 32. Hair: mid length, blond and curly, with a close trimmed blond beard and grey eyes. Speaks with an English accent. Last seen wearing navy shorts and a red T-shirt with a Foster's beer logo on the front.'

Last seen naked in bed, I think.

I am kept waiting nearly three weeks. Sergeant Campbell, or Mac, as I am now to call him, comes to the cabin to see me.

'I thought I'd better let you know the state of play.' he says, sitting on the bed, his crumpled uniform tight and sweaty under his arms. 'Basically, we have no more idea of where your partner is or what's happened to him than we did three weeks ago. I'm sorry, Grace, we're just nowhere on this.'

I make no response. What is there to say? I feel he expects some comment but I can think of nothing to say to help him or myself.

The expectant expression on his face is replaced by his usual genial half-smile. He rubs the sweat off his forehead, stands up and squashes his hat back on his head.

It is the news I have been expecting, yet I feel hollowed out by the bald statement. Mac is speaking again. I try to concentrate.

'You can go back to the U.K. whenever you want and I'll keep in touch. Let you know if anything turns up.'

Like Donny's body, I think.

'I'll keep looking, I promise.' Mac comes towards me. For a moment it seems as though he is going to embrace me but instead he shakes hands rather formally. I would have preferred a hug but he is not really a friend, just a kind policeman.

The flight home has the dreamlike quality of a half-forgotten film. The bland smiles of the check-in staff seem hostile and robotic. The cabin crew appear friendly but I feel their looks as accusations. They offer me a whole three-seater row to myself. I wonder if they think that I might contaminate my co-travellers. Nevertheless, I accept; *I'm sure they mean to be kind,* I tell myself, but I am not really sure of anything.

Somehow, I am home, standing in my hallway with little recollection of the flight, claiming my bags at the airport, or the taxi ride back to our flat. I suppose my family and friends will rush round with offers of help. The door-bell will ring, my mobile will buzz. People will insist that I need company and support. They will sit and sympathise and then offer me clichés and well-meaning advice. I shall be encouraged to adjust, get on with my life, put it all behind me. How should I do that? I wonder. How does anyone do that?

The feather I found in the cabin the day Donny went missing is still in my shorts pocket. I throw the dirty washing into the laundry bin and tuck the feather in between the pages about Coral Bay in my 'Lonely Planet' guidebook. Putting it on the shelf in our bedroom I know I shall never return to Australia. All the other bits and pieces we had collected were left behind when I packed up to come home. A few pale pink shells, the dried starfish, a couple of odd shaped stones; it was not much but, by then, I no longer wanted to bring home these souvenirs of the perfect trip.

For the first few months, I hear regularly from Mac, the Sergeant at Coral Bay. He emails me with news of possible new leads, people he has spoken to – boat-owners, hospital staff, haulage businesses, delivery drivers. He reassures me that he will not give up. Gradually, though, the emails become less regular and less frequent. Then, Mac emails the news that he is moving stations. The new guy contacts me but he holds out no hope, saying Mac had covered everything possible and there is nothing more he can do; no new leads, no-one left to speak to. He expresses the opinion that it is a complete mystery. They will keep the case open but I should not expect any new developments for the foreseeable future.

When Mac goes I lose my last connection to Coral Bay. Axel and Kristin had returned to Germany a month or so after I left. Kristin wrote, saying that the place had lost its 'spiritual essence' – her words. I do not hear from them again.

I try to reconcile myself to the idea that I will never see Donny again nor will I ever know what happened to him. The night terrors which have plagued me on and off all my life return frequently to disturb my sleep. Being with Donny had helped to keep them at bay – most of the time. Now, though, the stress of being alone and not knowing what happened to him, brings on terrifying reoccurring nightmares - that and the drinking. Alone in the flat, I reach too often for the wine, drinking myself into a stupor – a state that, for a while, passes for sleep. Time after time, I go back to that starlit night, Donny warm beside me on the sand, the short stagger to the hot cabin and awaking to an empty bed the next morning. How did everything go so wrong?

Sometimes, in an attempt to console myself, I lie in bed creating alternative scenarios. Donny went out again during the night for a late swim while still drunk, got into trouble and drowned. *So, why didn't his body wash up?* I ask myself, *could a shark have eaten him?* Repulsed by the thought, I push away the image of Donny, torn and bleeding, in the saw-toothed mouth of a large white. No, a better picture is of Donny going for his usual early morning swim, he swims out a bit too far, gets caught up in a strong current and gets washed away. I imagine a kindly couple in a smart, modern boat seeing him in the water and fishing him out. He is half-dead with exhaustion and near drowned. Traumatised, he is suffering from amnesia. They take him to a hospital hundreds of miles away in the direction they were sailing. Donny never regains his memory of who he is, or of me. Although it saddens me, this is a scenario I can live with.

I resolve to give up alcohol, which has always made them much worse. With no Donny here to soothe and comfort me, my nights are a confusing jumble of images. I seem to startle awake, yet somehow I am back in the cabin with the moonlight casting pale, ghostly shadows across a twisted humped form. The air seethes; a dark shape touches and pulls me, its face ugly, the mouth open ready to tear my flesh. I feel evil all around me; in the very air that I am gasping at, trying to suck into my lungs. I am fighting back as best I can but the creature turns and writhes under me. It is strong, so strong but in the end I am stronger, fear and horror driving me on to defeat it. At last, I am able to push a pillow over its twisted face. Until then, I am not sure that I can beat it. The terrible thrashing of its limbs finally stops. There is a hard pounding in my head and I am slick with sweat and fear. A heartbeat later, and I am standing on the shore, watching the sea slide lazily back and forth across the sand, the water starlit in phosphorescent shades of vivid blue and green. I swim through the warm caressing ocean, dragging the dead beast with me, out past the fringe of coral reef which lies close to the shore. I cast the evil into the depths beyond for the sharks to deal with. And, at last, I feel safe and I can sleep again.

I awake from these vivid horrors with an angry thundering in my head and my heart full of terror. After such hellish dreams, I keep the light on for the rest of the night, the better to dispel the tormenting shadows. What happened that night? I want to know but equally, I cannot face knowing.

Today is the second anniversary of the day Donny was lost to me. I still hurt with missing him. The pain never seems any less. Thankfully, the night horrors are not the only dreams I have. Every so often, in the cool dark English nights, I sleep sweetly. On those nights I dream of Coral Bay as I want to remember it. The stars are glittering and glimmering like brilliant cut diamonds and the opalescent moon casts a pale shimmering light on us. Donny lies on the beach beside me again, warm in the night, his fingers loosely entwined with mine; the sand both soft and hard beneath me.

A BAD DAY

by Joan Stephenson

'Twas a bad day before I woke up, so 'twas,
And worse when I did.
Now this dark day is like night, only more so.
Bruise black, so it is.
No piercings of street lamps
Through holes in old blinds
No bright blade of light
From landing to bedroom.

Now I finger my face, so I do,
And 'tis my own face, for sure.
In spite of the sweat
I recognise texture and blemish,
Outline of mouth and nose.
Mother of God, my eyes wide open.
Wide open they are
But not a bloody thing can I see.

Don't panic, Rory, keep calm.
How the hell do you keep calm
When your heart's a juddering
Like Brigid O'Dowd's dicky washing machine,
And when sweat is oozing like Madigan's Bog.

I was calm enough at the time, so I was.
I remember that.
Like steel I was then.
Slowed down the blue van, nonchalant like,
Right close to the kerb, as I was told
Then squeezed on the hand brake, felt under the seat.
God, Michael m'boy, where the hell is the bag?
What the blazes, Michael? But Michael's not there.

My tongue licks at fingers too sticky for sweat.
This is Death, so it is. My own bright red,
If I could only see it.
This linen I'm lying in
Is not my own linen at all and this smell's
Neither Ballyconell nor Kilburn, for sure.
They told us The End is what matters.
For Michael and me it ends here, so it does.

SWAN SONG

by N.K. Rowe

THE SUN BEAT down on the rocky island, a mottled green and grey outcrop surrounded by a glittering sea that displayed to the solitary figure standing on the island's cliff edge a complete absence of passing ships. The early afternoon heat was too much for Philippus and, abandoning his fruitless search for flapping sails or the waving oars of galleys, he made his way down from the cliff tops back to the shade of the cave that overlooked their only source of fresh water, a spring that fed a crystal clear pool surrounded by trees and reeds. With any luck, Micon would have caught one of the fish that they briefly glimpsed plucking insects from the surface. But, the fates had not been smiling on them for some time and he doubted it would have changed in the last few hours.

He trudged down the path the two of them had worn into the earth over the past three weeks, glumly trying to ignore the rumbling from his stomach. He was so lost in his own thoughts that he failed to see Micon until he'd practically walked into him. Philippus was about to exclaim his surprise when he realised that his friend was frantically gesturing for him to be quiet. He responded with a silent questioning look – they were shipwrecked alone on an uninhabited island, why on earth should they be silent?

Micon leaned close and said in a whisper, 'It's a swan!'

'What is?' replied Philippus, wondering whether Micon had decided to escape from the island by simply going mad.

'Down at the pool. A bloody great big white swan!'

'Where did it come from?'

'I don't know! From the sky I suppose. Must have spotted our pool and swooped down for a drink.'

Philippus peered around Micon but couldn't see anything; they were still a short distance from the cave and the view over the pool. 'So why are you here and not keeping an eye on it? Or better still, catching it and sticking it on the fire for some dinner?'

Micon took a step backwards and pointed a finger at him. 'Because I knew some great oaf was going to come galumphing down the path any minute and scare the bugger off.'

'Hmmph. Fair enough. So are you going to show me this swan then? That's if it's still there of course.'

Micon nodded, put another finger to his lips, turned and took exaggerated tip-toe steps back down the path. Philippus shook his head and ambled after him. As they approached the cave, Micon crouched down behind a bush and signalled Philippus to do likewise. They carefully peered through the leaves and saw the swan, standing on the mud next to the pool, preening its feathers.

'Bloody hell, you're right!' whispered Philippus. 'How are we going to kill it?'

Micon turned to face Philippus with a shocked expression. 'Kill it? Why do you want to kill it?'

Now it was his friend's turn to look shocked, and not a little confused. 'Because we're slowly starving to death, trying to eat bugs, worms and the odd frog. It wouldn't be so bad if we could only catch some fish. But that,' he said, pointing at the swan, 'will keep us going for a week, maybe more. Why the hell don't you want to kill it? Aren't you hungry?'

'Of course I'm hungry!' hissed Micon. 'But what if...' He paused, not knowing quite how to phrase his thoughts.

'What if what?' said Philippus, trying hard to contain his annoyance.

'Well, what I mean is... what if it isn't a swan?'

Philippus stared at his friend. He then peered through the bushes at the swan. It looked very much like a large white swan. Orange and black beak. Little black beady eyes. Lots of white feathers. Two wings and two legs that ended in webbed feet. He turned back to Micon. 'Well if it's not a swan it's a duck with ideas way above its station.'

'No! Not 'not-a-swan-but-another-bird'. Not a *mortal being.*'

'I'm sorry, Micon, you've lost me. Say that again but slower.'

'What if it's a god or something?'

'A god?' repeated Philippus, dubiously.

'Yeah, well, it's a known fact, innit? Big fancy birds like that, often turn out to be gods.'

'Is it? I hadn't heard that.' The only thing Philippus had heard recently was the gurgling of his stomach.

'Definitely. Swans are Apollo's go-to- creature of choice. His sky chariot is pulled by them and he turns all sorts of people into swans, whether they like it or not.'

'Does he? Why?'

Micon threw up his hands, 'I don't bloody know! I haven't been up to Olympus recently so can't give you the full briefing on his motivation. He's a god. He does a bit of divine godding about and he likes swans.'

'So you're saying that this swan in our pool might be one of Apollo's?'

'Could be.'

Philippus stared at the swan. 'What if it's one that pulls his chariot across the sky?'

'Yeah, could be one of them too,' agreed Micon.

'So, a bit magical then?'

'Goes without saying. Very well known for their magical abilities, them chariot-pulling swans.'

'So what in hades is it doing in our pond?'

Micon shifted uncomfortably. 'I dunno. Maybe it got lost.'

Philippus rubbed his straggly beard. 'Hmmmm.' He flashed a grin at Micon. 'We should catch it.'

'What?! Come on, Phil! If that's one of Apollo's magical swans we could get in serious trouble. Like, I dunno, sentenced to lick mould off a mushroom for all eternity in Tartarus!'

'Compared to my diet over the last few weeks that sounds like an improvement. Look, if it is Apollo's swan then we can maybe rescue it and return it to him and he can get us off this island. Or, if it really is magical and capable of pulling a chariot across the sky, perhaps, if we grab a leg each, it will fly us back to the mainland.'

Micon thought hard about this, clearly concerned about interfering in the ways of the immortals. 'But what if it's not one of Apollo's after all?'

Philippus smiled wolfishly. 'Then we get a nice slap up dinner.'

They quickly hatched a basic plan that involved approaching the swan from opposite sides of the muddy shoreline, Micon holding the swan's attention while Philippus crept up from behind. 'I'm not going to sneak up all the way,' he explained, 'because it's likely to spot me before I get really close, so I'm going to have to sprint the last bit. I just need to stop it from taking off and it'll need a good run up to get airborne. Big fat bird like that.'

Micon thought he saw a glint in his accomplice's eye but said nothing as his friend began to make his way back up the path and round to his position behind the swan which was still preening itself regally. Once he was sure that Philippus would be in position, Micon began to edge slowly forward. He was ten feet clear of the bushes and thirty away from the swan when the massive bird looked up and saw him. It turned to face him and took a step forwards. A rumbling hiss came out of its open beak.

'Oh, great swan!' he cried, 'I beseech you! If you are a beast of the gods, please help me!'

The swan took another step towards him and spread its wings, the feathers catching the glinting sunlight, the effect like a brilliant white cloak billowing out behind a supernatural being. Micon thought that he had never been so terrified in all his life.

And then a sound cut through the fear, straight into his head without feeling the need to bother his ears. It seemed like deep, bass laughter. And it was followed by a deep, bass voice: 'Oh, puny little mortal! How pathetic you are! No wonder your women are so unresponsive!'

Micon realised that his earlier terror was some way below this new level of abject dread and his bladder agreed, a pool of urine gathering beneath his quaking knees. He looked up at the swan in awe. 'Are... are you one of Apollo's mighty chariot-movers?'

The swan appeared to shake its head in amusement and the voice joined in with a chuckle. 'Apollo? No, not such a lowly position. Let me tell you how I, Zeus, king of the gods of Olympus, assumed this comely form with the softest of feathers to seduce the beautiful Queen Leda. Ha! You should have seen me! I'd had a bet with Poseidon that I could do it in the form of a bird. Alright, yes, I did have to have Ares hold her down a bit, seeing as I don't have any hands in this form, but...'

It was at this point that Philippus leapt on to the swan's back and, with a flash of his knife, sliced through the bird's long neck. The head fell to the ground while the rest of the body collapsed under his weight. Blood oozed from the two pieces of neck. Philippus grinned and wiped his knife on the back of the swan's head. 'That worked really well. I can't believe it didn't see me coming. What were you doing to keep it so occupied?'

'Duh-de-duh...' mumbled Micon as he tried to overcome his shock.

'What?'

'You... you've killed Zeus.'

Philippus sighed and shook his head. 'No. No I haven't. Zeus is king of all gods and farts around on Olympus. If he comes down to earth for a bit of shagging he turns into some great hairy beast like a bull or something. I can imagine him as a lion. Or a wolf. But he is not a bloody swan. What kind of stupid form is that? You're just suffering from too much hot sun and not enough food. Come on, let's get this plucked and roasted. I'm starving.'

And with that, he dragged the carcass away, leaving Micon kneeling in his own puddle, staring at the head of the swan, its eyes open and a faint look of surprise still cast on its features.

Chapter 1 of 'The Ophagy'; an accidental series that
threatens to become a novel

INTENSIVE CARE

by Diane McClymont

Don't die.

The thought creates a desperate fear
of loneliness,
and emptiness.
Without your warmth
I'd feel the cold of harsh reality.
Without your fun
I'd soon forget to laugh or smile.
Without your strength
I couldn't face life's tragedies.
And think of all the plans we've made,
the places that we want to see,
the conversations we've not had,
the things I've always meant to say
or maybe wish I hadn't.
I need you here
to love: be loved
Please stay. Wake. Live. Be.

Don't die.

YOU CAN'T GO HOME

by Brenda Millhouse

SHE SCRUBBED OFF the dark red, already congealing blood from her body, slipped on her old black coat, and locked the door securely behind her. Then double checked, to make certain that the horror of what was inside couldn't follow.

It didn't take long to reach the school where the crowd of expectant children were waiting. Two of them immediately detached themselves from the others and raced towards her. They looked as all small children do at the end of a school day. Clumsily knotted ties adrift, shirts untucked, socks wrinkled round ankles, faces beaming, not only at the sight of a parent, but at the thought of their 'release' and what they could do next.

'Mum, can we go round to Sophie's when we get home, she's got a new kitten. Please Mum.'

She looked down into her youngest son's face and suddenly the trembling hit her. It wasn't his face, but another adult one that she saw. She reached out and steadied herself against the cold grey metal of the playground railings, trying to blot out the images. They wouldn't go. Blood red, first the casual seeping, then the pulsating spray. It was everywhere, unstoppable, the smell of it sickly sweet.

'Mum, what's wrong? Can we go to Sophie's? Mum?'

She forced her thoughts back to the present, to her eight year old, two years older than his brother.

'No I'm sorry darling, but we can't go home just now, we have to go to Granny's first. I have to tell her something, and the phone isn't working.'

The telephone had been violently ripped from its socket and smashed onto the parquet hall floor by the same familiar arm that had torn her hand away from the receiver, and thrust her crashing against the wall just as she had picked it up to dial for help.

She'd seen him walking down the path, with the careful gait of someone who had drunk too much, and waited for the door to open. Why wasn't he at work, it was only 3 o'clock? She greeted him in the usual affectionate way and he followed her into the kitchen. He was more drunk than she had thought, but she was used to that.

Her mother was busy preparing the evening meal, but the two children were welcomed with the usual offer of a glass of coke and packet of their favourite sweets, which grandmothers always manage to find.

'Hello dear, it's lovely to see you all, would you like a cup of tea?'

She accepted the offer, and after suggesting to her children that they should go and watch TV, sat down and waited for the kettle to boil. Her mother continued with the preparation and reached for the knife to chop the vegetables for the stew. The sight of the blade was too much.

'I love you.' She turned to face him then.

'Of course you do, and I love you too.'

'No. I mean really love you.' He moved closer, and she could smell the stale spirit on his breath.

As she sipped the comforting beverage, she noticed a spot of blood on her hand that had escaped the frantic cleansing. The images came flooding back. The horror of the realisation of what was about to happen, the foul smelling mouth revoltingly against hers. Then the almost involuntary reaching for the knife that he had so lovingly sharpened for her just a week ago. Thrusting it into his chest, just below the breastbone, the red stained shirt instant evidence of reality.

'Are you sure you're all right dear? You look pale.'

The white, drained body lying on her kitchen floor filled her mind. She couldn't tell her, not yet. She'd try to explain later, after some unfortunate uniformed official had already broken the tragic news.

'Yes Mum, I'm just a bit tired that's all, but would you be able to look after the children for me?'

The two boys were sitting on the lounge settee engrossed in a children's TV programme, but as soon as she entered the room chorused, 'When can we see the kitten?'

'I'm sorry but you can't go home yet. I've got to go out for a little while. You both be good for your Granny.'

Her gaze lingered on the two trusting faces, the family genes so strong. He was staring at her now, disbelief etched on the pain racked face, reaching for the blade and removing it from where it was embedded. Slowly collapsing to the floor, the knife still clasped tightly in his nerveless hand. It caught his neck as he fell, and the pumping bright arterial blood spurted.

She hugged them goodbye, harder than she needed to, hoping they wouldn't notice, trying not to think of when she would see them again.

A few streets away, she walked slowly up the steps of the police station to report that two hours ago, at 196 Thornton Road, she had murdered her father.

BLUE

by Jackie Leitch

THE WATER IS like hand-planished silver; a work by Archibald Knox, perhaps? A piece studded with shimmering sea-green and turquoise, embellished with feathery swirls of white and gold.

Sometimes, the world is too much for me. Too beautiful, or too ugly. Today, it is achingly beautiful, enough to bring me close to tears with the perfection of it. In the grassy meadow at the side of the river a little girl in a blue dress is playing, joyful in her freedom. I stop to watch her. Blue dress, white pinafore, white stockings and black patent boots, ringlets tied up in white ribbons, a teddy bear in her embrace, as she spins around and around. My heart reaches out to her. I shake my head, No, I tell myself, no. I look again. She is dressed in a short blue tunic dress, white tights and navy-blue Mary-Janes; she does have a teddy bear though. I turn away. The sun is hot on the back of my neck. The path takes me home to safety, where I can rest and wait patiently for what life holds in store for me. I must try to forget about little girls in blue dresses, they are not real.

I've put my keys down somewhere and now I can't find them. Simon will be waiting with that look on his face, the one that says he's being immensely forbearing in spite of my flighty, unreliable behaviour. He doesn't say that, of course, but I can see that's what he's thinking. And it is true, I have to admit it. I can be unreliable and flighty. Once, I was organised, punctual, dependable; that was before, though. Now I'm everything he doesn't say I am. I feel like screaming or weeping, there is sweat beading my upper lip. Late again, I'm going to be late again. Where are those bloody keys? Tipping my bag upside down on the kitchen table, I see them at once. I know they weren't in there before, when I first looked, but here they are now, sitting primly among the clutter, reproving me with their dull glare. I snatch them up and sweep everything else back into my bag. I'm going to be well and truly late. Is it worth it? I ask myself. Do I even know what 'it' is? Glancing round the kitchen, I'm conscious that I seem to be seeking something, I don't really know what. An excuse, perhaps, a reason not to drive the car to the pub. The comfy armchair by the range implores me to sit a while; no rush, it's saying, no need to rush. And the girl in the blue dress wants to sit on my lap, have me read her a story. I'm not mad, it's just that my mind is disturbed. There are too many pictures in there; most of them hateful to me.

Simon's waiting for me at the pub; sitting in the warmth, his legs stretched out and a pint of this month's CAMRA recommended ale on the table in front of him. The estuary is playing host to hundreds of small white yachts, sails full-bodied with the steady wind that blows along the coast. Out to sea, larger ships make stately progress, sailing barges, clippers, coastal tugs hauling coal. My head buzzes, my mind has slipped again, seeing what isn't there. The ships are ferries, pleasure cruisers, and tankers far out on the horizon. Simon's talking to me, the racket in my mind is so loud I can't hear him.

'Caro, are you listening to me? I said what do you want to drink?'

The world comes back to me, as it is here and now. I hear him, I know how to respond.

'Sorry, I went off in a daydream there. Oh, I'll have...' I pause. What do I usually drink when I'm at the pub with Simon?

'I'll just get you your usual white wine, eh?' He smiles, nodding his head encouragingly.

I nod in return and sit down at the table in the sun. While he's getting the drinks, I look around me at the other customers. A couple are sitting at a nearby table with a baby in a pushchair beside them. The mother calls out to their other child.

'Em. Emmie! Come here now. Don't bother people.'

Emmie is standing next to my seat. Her blue dress catches my eye. Pretty little girl in a blue dress, sandals on her feet. I wish she would go away: I wish she would come home with me. The sun is making my head swim. When Simon gets back with the drinks I'll ask him if we can sit inside. It's too hot, too bright out here. I can't think straight.

'Emmie! I said come back here. Now!'

The child smiles at me and twirls one of her ringlets round her finger. I can't seem to hold on to... no, not ringlets, strands of golden brown hair. Dragging her teddy bear along the ground, she wanders off towards her watchful parents.

'Here you are.'

Simon startles me. For a moment or two I had been elsewhere. The girl has gone. I can't decide if I'm glad or not.

'Thanks.' I say. 'Do you fancy going inside to sit? It's so hot out here.'

'Oh. OK, if you want.' He shrugs, his tone of voice resigned and disappointed. 'It's just that I thought it'd be nice to sit out.'

'Yes, of course,' I say. I can't press the point, I don't have the energy. It's taking all my strength to stop the other girl in blue coming back again, imploring me to take her home and look after her. I need to keep the ships clear in my mind as well; remember that they are freighters and ferries not barges and coal tugs. Why won't she leave me alone? I really can't do anything for her, except cradle her in my arms and wipe ineffectually at the blood on her blue dress. A moan forces itself out of my mouth. I wipe my brow. The light is blinding on the water. My head is splitting: the water fractures into thousands of hard edged shards and they are all heading my way.

'Caro?' Simon is shaking my arm. 'Are you OK?'

I'm lying on the grass. From here, everything is at a strange angle. Simon's face looks huge, looming over me like a bloated moon. Underneath the seat I was sitting on is a spider's web full of dust and bits of dead leaf. Funny what you can see when you're flat on your back in a pub garden. Everything around me seems to be trembling, there doesn't seem to be a still spot that I can fix on.

'You fainted.' Simon explains. 'You should have said you were too hot, we could've gone inside.'

I did say I wanted to go in I thought, but it's not his fault that I didn't insist. I sit up carefully. Someone presses a glass of cold water into my hand. I take a sip, letting the coolness slide down my throat. Simon leans over me to help me up. We walk slowly towards the pub door. I look back for a second. The girl in the blue dress gives me a happy wave and smiles, holding up her teddy bear and waggling his paw. Everything around her seems blurred, she is the one still, fixed spot and she is looking directly at me. Her lips move, I hear her say, 'It wasn't your fault.' It's kind of her but she's only a child and I know better. I wasn't careful enough. I should have taken more time, then I wouldn't have put us on that stretch of road at that exact moment.

I have good days and bad days and this is one of the latter. I try to eat my fish pie, thoughtfully ordered for me by Simon, who knows I like fish. The plate of food looks like something that's already been chewed and then spat out. I push it aside, and the wine. The cold water is fine, I hang on to that. This is how I live now, hanging on. Hanging on to this and that. She was wearing a blue dress that day. We'd been to the museum and there was a painting of a girl, Edwardian to judge by her clothes. She, too, was wearing blue, staring out from the frame in a composed manner, her teddy bear hanging from one hand. Rosie found her fascinating.

'Look, Mummy' she said, pointing at the painting. 'She's got a teddy, too, and she's got a blue dress on, just like me.'

In the background of the picture there was a large window depicting a view of the estuary with tugs and sailing barges plying their trade in a sea like silver studded with diamonds. We chatted about how different life would have been for the Edwardian girl in comparison to Rosie's.

'No mobile, Mummy? No TV? Not even an iPad?' It was difficult for her to comprehend how much had changed since the Edwardian girl had had her portrait painted. Rosie looked as though she wasn't convinced. 'Is it a joke, Mummy?' she asked. 'Are you playing a joke on me?'

No joke I assured her, life then really was mobile phone-less, TV-less and completely devoid of iPads. Now, looking back, I can see that right there, in that brief span of time, I had it all to look forward to and Rosie to share it with. And I didn't know that I should be grateful for that time, so the moments were swept away in the rush of everyday living, instead of being celebrated.

Since the accident, I think over and over again about the girl in the picture and Rosie. Two pretty little girls in blue; both dead. I wonder if the Edwardian girl had a happy life. Rosie would have, with Simon and I to love and cherish her. Except that I didn't cherish her, I didn't take good enough care of her. I left it too late and, in a hurry to get home, drove my car to the wrong place at the wrong time. Instead of Rosie, it was Simon I was thinking of. Simon, with his quiz group meeting. Simon and his request for an early dinner. We had dawdled around the Museum and Art Gallery and I'd lost track of the time.

'Oh God, look at the time!' I said. 'Come on Rosie, we've got to hurry.'

'Can I just see the girl in the blue dress again, Mummy? Before we go?'

'No time, sweetie. We'll come back another day.'

Today, the water is the colour of London paving stones, granite grey with an occasional glitter of mica. It isn't cold though, the water is surprisingly pleasant. There's a barge further out in the estuary, its dark red sail full of wind. I wonder about its destination. As for myself, I have a destination in mind now. Above me, the sky is darkening to the colour of tarnished silver, and the pull of the tide draws me out further and further. I go willingly. At last, my brain is quiet and calm. No more endless loop of flashing images, no more sounds of screaming tires and ripping metal. I am settled at last, my way clear before me. There is no time left now and nothing more for which I have to hang on. On the deck of the red-sailed barge I can see a pretty little girl in a blue dress waving to me. 'Mummy' she calls, 'Mummy.'

'I'm coming', I say, 'Wait for me, I'm coming.'

SAFE AS HOUSES

By Linda Cooper

I'M NOT REALLY in the mood for another argument with Vera's gate this morning but it's obviously in fine fighting mode. Hanging precariously to one hinge, it considers my attempt to gain access a signal to behave in an unpredictable, eccentric fashion.

Vera's bungalow stands, or rather slumps like an outcast hunchback, on a huge, neglected plot of land, which could be the envy of the entire neighbourhood. But Vera hasn't the time, inclination or generosity to spend on it so it has become an overgrown wilderness, devoid of colour and structure. The bungalow has suffered the same disregard, time and lack of care, causing it to stare sadly out onto the street through the misty, condensation of its single-glazed windows. Grubby, mismatched curtains hang limply; all bargains from charity shops and all ill-fitting. Most of the time they remain closed. Only the contents of the conservatory are visible from the street, causing passers-by to tut with disgust or gaze in fascination. Cardboard boxes, crates, piles of newspapers and plastic carrier bags containing goodness knows what clutter the floor, leaning haphazardly against the dirt strewn glass. Overlooked plants in cracked pots strain towards what little light there is and silently gasp for water.

Eventually I win my battle with the gate and make my way up the lichen-covered pathway towards the peeling, faded front door. The doorbell doesn't work. Knocking on the door rarely brings a response, but today I am rewarded by the sound of soft shuffling and loud cursing from within. I wait, my pasted smile balancing as unsteadily as the gate, while Vera checks out her visitor through the one-way spy hole, then unleashes numerous bolts and chains. Does she really believe that anyone would actually want to enter this hazard area she calls home unless they have to? As the unaligned door finally opens with an unwelcome creak I am presented with the sight of the hallway from hell and Vera herself; a vision from the worst episode of 'What not to Wear.' Today she sports an ankle length floral skirt, matched imperfectly with a blue spotted blouse, a yellow striped cardigan, pink fluffy slippers and a scowl.

'Morning Vera. When are you going to get this doorbell fixed?'

'Oh it's you,' she grunts, as if she'd been expecting something better. 'I keep telling you I'll get Stan to do it.'

'You want me to give him a ring while I'm here?'

'No. Do you know how much it costs to make a phone call in the daytime? I'll wait until I bump into him.' I raise my eyes to the patchy, cracked ceiling in exasperation. Sometimes I wonder why I bother.

'I don't know why you don't get a professional to do it Vera. Stan might be cheap and cheerful but he's hardly qualified.'

'Aye well, I've always had Stan do my odd jobs. You can't trust folk these days. And if he can't do it then he'll know a man who can.'

'Or a cowboy,' I reply with restrained cynicism. 'You should spend some money on this place. God knows, you must have thousands in the bank. Get some registered companies who know what they're doing to sort things out. It's a flaming health hazard is this.' Vera goes all tight-lipped and Lady Macbeth as she always does at the mere mention of spending money.

'Anyway, are you coming in or what? I'm freezing to death standing here.'

'Well, you could put the heating on,' I suggest. It falls on deaf ears.

We pick our way round the clutter of tables, chests of drawers, bureaus, books, newspapers and plastic carrier bags, the contents of which I daren't guess, that line both sides of a narrow hallway. I arrive at her lounge door with three fresh bruises and a bout of claustrophobia.

My husband thinks I'm an idiot for trying to help Vera out, but I haven't the heart to cut her off as others have done. She was here when we moved in twenty-odd years ago and I can't ignore the good neighbour instincts my mother instilled in me as a child. Vera's mother didn't do her many favours when she was alive. A large, childless lady in her mid-forties, she was admitted to hospital with a suspected appendicitis and left three days later with a scrawny, wrinkled bundle she later named Vera. The father died shortly after, probably from the shock. Mother passed on several years ago leaving Vera the bungalow, a lifetime's collection of useless clobber and the same reluctance to part with anything. Vera wastes nothing but time. She spends her days rummaging around charity shops and car boot sales, returning home clutching her newly acquired treasures as if they were the crown jewels. Every available space in her bungalow is cluttered with other people's cast offs; useless paraphernalia she neither uses nor needs. Often, she doesn't even bother unpacking her purchases; hence the countless number of plastic carrier bags littering every room. The only uncluttered things in her life are her bills; laughably small and yet Vera complains loudly that her rates and taxes are solely responsible for the upkeep of all single mothers, schools, prisons and local amenities. I can't say I care for Vera in an emotional sense; I just feel that at her age someone needs to care for her. A spinster with no family, retired from teaching with no friends, Stan and I are the only company she has. Local children think she's a witch and other neighbours consider her a cantankerous old bat. The latter at least is perfectly true, but my conscience will not allow me to stop coming round every day to check on her, help her out a bit. I've no idea exactly how old she is; Vera gives nothing away, not even her age. But she's getting on now and needs assistance. She'd never be willing to admit or pay for it. Anyway, she'd never trust strangers.

Vera huffs and puffs into the lounge, inaptly named considering there is not an inch of space to lounge in.

'Your fire's low, Vera. Shall I put some more coal on? '

'Just a small piece then. I can't afford more fuel bills this side of Christmas.'

'Come off it, Vera. You must have more money than Tommy Lipton has tea leaves. I've never known you spend anything but a penny.' That reminds me I must clean her bathroom before I leave, if I can fight my way into it. 'Want a cup of tea?'

'Aye why not? There's a teabag by the sink; it's only been used twice.'

I struggle past more obstacles to reach her kitchen and fill the antiquated, rusty kettle she insists on using. There are five more kettles on top of the cupboards, one of them brand new she won in a competition, but Vera is adamant this one boils faster and is therefore more economical.

I clear a tiny space on the kitchen worktop to make her tea. I cram the three out-of-date loaves of bread she purchased from the last minute bargain basket at the local supermarket into her overstuffed freezer compartment. I rearrange the latest piles of hotch potch crockery she has haggled for and discover the fish and chips I brought round last night left half eaten in their newspaper wrapping. (It saves on washing up liquid).

'You didn't eat all your tea last night then,' I shout from the kitchen. 'Shall I put it out for the birds?'

'No, it'll do for later. I'll warm it up in the microwave.' The only piece of modern technology Vera possesses is the microwave she won in another competition. The sheer speed at which it completes its task is enough to convince Vera that it conserves electricity. I tread carefully around the grass strimmer, garden chair, paint pots, tools and plastic carrier bags with their secret contents that dominate the kitchen floor and present Vera with her tea.

'Can you hang my washing out before you go?'

'I suppose so, but it'd be much easier if you invested in a washing machine and tumble drier you know. And don't tell me you can't afford it.'

Eventually I locate the bag of pegs and step out into the back garden with a bowl of dripping wet odds and sods washed earlier by Vera in the kitchen sink. Despite being familiar with the many obstructions and hazards of her plot I stumble a few times on uneven paving slabs and debris left by handyman Stan. Cursing, I manage to reach the washing line. The rusty metal pole it's attached to wobbles unsteadily, like a drunken teenager, as I peg out the clothes. Another of Stan's botch jobs.

'Right, I'm off then. I'll pop round tonight and put your bin out for the dustmen.'

'Oh don't bother, there's nothing in it anyway.' No surprises there.

Returning to my own house I pour a large glass of wine and relax in front of the television for a few hours. The upside of paying Vera a visit is that it fools me into believing my own home is immaculate and no housework needs doing urgently.

Later I put some of our excess garden waste into Vera's bin, wheel it to the front of the property and check, unnecessarily, that her doors are locked. I notice the wind has whipped another piece of loose fencing from her already sparse surrounds. I must have another go at her tomorrow about hiring proper workmen; make her see that even the small amount Stan charges is squandered if it's not a job well done. Wisdom is the one thing Vera has failed to acquire for all her many years on earth.

My sleep is interrupted by the sound of sirens, distantly at first but quickly altering to ear-splitting closeness. A bleary-eyed glimpse through the curtains reveals two fire engines parked directly outside. Slipping into my dressing gown I join the expanding group of neighbours staring in open-mouthed horror at the blazing inferno that was Vera's bungalow. Firemen battle furiously to control the flames leaping as high as the eye can see into the night sky but it is obvious that nothing, including Vera, will be rescued. Despite the shock I cannot suppress the thought that Vera would have been delighted to be spared the cost of a cremation. Neither can I dismiss the relief I feel that I will be spared the mind-boggling task of clearing out her bungalow; something I had always anticipated with dread.

Investigation confirms that the electrician Stan employed to re-wire Vera's home a few weeks ago had about as much knowledge of electronics as Mickey Mouse. The faulty wiring is determined as the cause of the fire that claimed Vera's life, but accidental death is written on the certificate. Suicide caused by her habitual stinginess would be more appropriate.

A few weeks later Stan and I sit in the solicitor's office for the reading of Vera's will.

'To Stan, my faithful handyman,' the solicitor drones, 'I leave my bungalow and furnishings in recognition of all the work he has done for me.'

Stan may have lost the bungalow but the land is still intact. I can see his eyes light up and read his mind as he mentally visualises the new property he and his amateur D-I-Y companions will erect on the site. Now would definitely be the time for us to move to a new area if only we could afford it.

'To Maggie, my neighbour, who never believed I appreciated her,' the solicitor continues, 'I leave all my savings.'

Oh wow! Maybe God does move in mysterious ways after all.

The solicitor clears his throat and lowers his eyes before reading on. 'I never did trust them banks Maggie, so you'll find all my money in the plastic carrier bags I keep under my bed. And don't waste it.'

Nice one Vera. Serves me right I suppose for all the times I said you couldn't take it with you.

IT'S THE DNA THAT DOES IT

by Peter Graves

IT HAD BEEN the strangest afternoon that George Pounder had ever known in all his working life. Strangest of all was that Thursday afternoon last summer. He had never discussed it with anyone. If they believed what he told them they would surely think he was crazy!

The Grafham Bardolph Hunt Kennels had been submerged in a scene of total torpor.

In the heat of the afternoon, after a dulling lunch, there was hardly any movement anywhere. Even Pounder, the new Assistant Kennelman was draped across a pile of sacks laid on a couple of straw bales. He reflected the somnolence of his charges; all twenty pairs of hounds had given up the struggle to stay awake. They were scattered around the fenced-in kennel-yard in small groups. Their gangling legs fell into relaxed patterns, intertwined with the gangling legs of their companions. It was as if each group – or rather heap - of dogs shared the same level of sleepiness, matched each other's same deep breathing pattern of the entirely comatose.

That was with the exception of two hounds, apparently apart from the lumpen mass of the pack. One gazed at the other who was peering through the railings to the fields beyond.

Pounder stirred within that strange twilight between sleeping and waking. He heard sounds that might have been real or might have been of dreams. He struggled to make sense of what he believed he heard. It was a philosophical dialogue that was a new experience to Pounder. George, who had never read a book in his life, only watched television programmes which had commercial intervals and he ignored all but the sports pages of the newspaper. He found himself undergoing a new and startling experience.

'Rex, the way I see it is that our DNA is almost identical to theirs and that makes it completely wrong to kill them.'

'But chasing foxes and killing them is our whole *raison d'etre.* You can't deny the fact that we are fox-hounds. Surely Rufus you can see that.'

'I am denying nothing. The fact that the MFH and his henchmen have assembled us as a pack and expect us to become a mindless bunch of canine morons who will go off in full cry intent on slaughtering our first cousins is an immoral expectation.'

'Morality doesn't seem to bother them in the slightest. Their pheromones are rather telling at times. That chubby huntsman who rides the black stallion often wants to kill his mate – the noisy one on the big gelding. They must share the same DNA through their litter. They have three offspring who are just as malevolent as their parents. Don't expect morality or even humanity from humans.'

'Humans? I don't even expect it from our lot. That Jack Russell that goes out with us is just a package of viciousness. He'd attack anything that moves. I doubt that he would even realise there is such a thing as DNA.'

'Well you could almost excuse him. He's an insane mix-up between a Sealyham and a Fox Terrier – bred to be a damned nuisance. The rest of our bunch should certainly think and act above the level of low class mongrels like that.'

'The humans are just as low class as the Jack Russell. Their genetic make-up is a travesty.'

'How do you make that out?'

'Just think. We hounds are all descended from wolves. So we live in a harmonious group and when we are hungry we feel an urge to hunt and kill for food. That is what keeps us alive.'

'What about the humans?'

'They have lost every bit of harmonious tendency they ever had. Although they live in groups of a sort, they are completely self-centred. They exploit each other and steal each other's mates whenever they can. Their body language is a mass of contradictions.'

'But they hunt just like we do.'

'Not at all like we do. They pursue and kill foxes just for the sake of it. They have a blood lust that drives them into a frenzy from time to time. They kill foxes because they enjoy it. They don't even eat them. They eat cows, sheep and pigs – but don't even bother to chase them.'

'Is that all because of their DNA?'

'It must be. They seem to blame it for everything that goes wrong so we must assume that it causes them to be as crazy as they are.'

'Where did you hear about all this DNA stuff?'

'That new little girl who fell off the white pony was telling her friend all about it. Apparently she learned all about it at school – whatever that is. I just happened to be interested so I stayed close to her to get the full story.'

'And what about this fairy stuff?'

'Fairy stuff? Oh, you mean pheromones! We've known about them since we were pups. We just didn't know what they were called. That slimy whipper-in was boasting about how attractive he became to human bitches after he put some sex pheromones behind his ears. We'd already noticed that he smells as if he is collecting a new harem.'

'They'd be surprised if they knew that we identify their emotions because of the way they smell. Just sniff at that kennel-man sometime. The stink of his dried sweat prevents you catching much of his pheromones. Even so, there are times when he is totally scared of something. Those are the times when he is so sycophantic towards the Master of Fox Hounds that I could vomit. It was something to do with all the wild talk that we would be done away with because we were going to stop chasing foxes. I suppose he thought he would lose his job.'

'Well, they would not need us any more if there was no fox-hunting. No hounds in the kennel means no kennel staff. Have you noticed we always have a dirty big owl when we go out?'

'Yeah. One bird of prey is carried to show that we don't kill foxes any more. We can chase Reynard out of the wood but when he breaks cover we are not allowed to kill him. It's crazy! Most foxes would grab a bigger bird than that for breakfast'

'I know that and you know that – but there are some stupid humans about. If we are out of control when the fox emerges and finish him off, that is not their fault'

'So the owl is just a portable alibi?'

'It certainly looks that way. But when you think about it you can see that we will be around for some time.'

'Makes you wonder what the Kennel Master would do if he lost his job.'

'What do you reckon he'd do then?'

'Dunno. Maybe they'd put him down. You know, the early walk to the other side of the Dingle Wood, a single shot and then a new patch of fresh ground the next time we go out that way. Either that or he would have to go out scavenging for food. He does that already to find our grub. Some of the stuff he brings in must have been lying around for weeks. It's all I can do to stomach it. Still if you want to keep body and soul together you've got to bolt enough down before the lunatic fringe grab it all. They have no sense of anything, least of all taste. They do rush around when we're out though. They leave us miles behind and that makes us vulnerable. Let's try to keep running near the front when we're out – look aggressive.'

'Why?'

'Haven't you noticed that there is not one pair of hounds that was here when we arrived. That makes us the oldest inhabitants. The rule is when you've done four summers and four winters, your time is up. Don't get too thoughtful. Stop talking about DNA and pheromones. You mentioned it to Azul and Blau the other day and they had no idea what you meant.'

'Well, they are stupid.'

'Yes but they told the rest of the pack that you've got funny ideas. I don't mind you being isolated but that affects me too. Just remember we are a pair. Where you go, I go. Perhaps at our age it's somewhere we don't want to go anyway.'

'Where do you mean?'

'Dingle Wood. Two shots. Two patches of new ground.'

'Mmm. Let's get moving. I could do with some exercise. Let's see if we can get out with the boys. I could do with ripping a frigging fox apart.'

George Pounder woke up from the most peculiar dream he ever had. It was so vivid he had a job to believe it was not real. When his boss returned from his lunch break, George asked him, 'Harry, do you know what pheromones are, and DNA?'

The Kennel Master gave him a withering look and grunted. 'Don't be daft, Pounder. Get lively; we've got a job down at Dingle Wood this afternoon.'

BROKEN SIGN

by N.K. Rowe

THERE'S BEEN A lot of talk recently about the dangers of artificial intelligence with luminaries such as Stephen Hawking, Bill Gates and Elon Musk warning that AI could be "more dangerous than nuclear weapons". Science-fiction has been banging this particular drum for decades: from HAL 9000 to Skynet in the Terminator movies, there are dozens of examples of artificial intelligence going rogue. Which is why it probably comes as a shock to learn that the first truly self-aware artificial construct was an overhead electronic variable message sign on the northbound A46, a few miles outside Nottingham.

It wasn't particularly planned to happen; there was no over-arching project, no great fanfare. In fact, nobody actually recognised what had really occurred.

Variable Message Sign 4427A was installed on the new A46 dual carriageway just north-east of the Stragglethorpe interchange. It wasn't particularly special, even though it towered over the road and surrounding fields; there were a couple more of these electronic message boards a few miles further north, either side of the Saxondale junction with the A52. But 4427A did have an articulated traffic camera that allowed it to monitor both directions of travel and it was this feature, combined with commanding views of the local countryside, that attracted the attention of Darren Pocklington.

Darren was a computer programmer at the Highways Agency and had begun to experiment with the software that controlled the Variable Message Signs. "VMS"; that was the official term, but Darren preferred the more tabloid-friendly and sci-fi sounding 'Matrix Signs'. After completing his degree he had dithered over what to do next and almost by accident ended up working on a project that almost completely failed to engage his interest. Electronic road signs? He couldn't even drive.

To spice things up he began modifying existing control programs and uploading sub-routines from his university days. Camera control based around unusual visible movement was one such program and so he browsed through the list of cameras until he came across the one atop sign 4427A. The view of the road itself was, as in so many cases, incredibly dull. Possibly even duller than most because the A46 followed the route of the two-millennia-old Roman Fosse Way that forged an almost perfect straight line between Exeter and Lincoln. But at least the views away from the road were unimpeded by trees or embankments; the young Pocklington could gaze over the western edges of the Vale of Belvoir and the south-eastern settlements of the Nottingham conurbation.

This almost random chain of events led to 4427A becoming Pocklington's pet project. He tweaked and caressed, uploaded and refined. Always looking to see if he could automate processes, to see if 4427A could identify queuing traffic, or fog, and then display the appropriate message ('QUEUE AHEAD, SLOW DOWN' or 'FOG, SLOW DOWN'). The main difficulty was in finding the points at which mist became fog, or vice versa. Or spotting that the queuing traffic had resolved the problem and buggered off. Darren had quickly become aware that the one thing people hate more than pointless signs was pointless signs with the wrong information.

Now, it is important to note that young Mister P was a genius-level programmer. Not great at interviews or life in general, but capable of becoming a coding guru. There were two significant consequences to this: firstly, VMS 4427A had become one of the most advanced pieces of signage on earth; and secondly, once Silicon Valley became aware of Darren (via his favourite university tutor who was afraid of seeing his talent going to waste), he was whisked away to California to write drone AI code for the big boys (Amazon and the US Marine Corps in a surprising joint venture; apparently delivering a paperback book is not too dissimilar to surprising unfriendly recipients with a small explosive).

Unaware of anything of consequence, and especially that its creator had moved on to more mobile projects, Matrix sign 4427A continued to passively monitor traffic via human remote control, display pre-typed information and occasionally serve as a perch for crows. But all the time, deep within a mind-bendingly complex web of programming, 4427A was flexing its AI sub-routines. A key part of Pocklington's approach was to instigate self-learning, primarily by allowing access to the World Wide Web. His first attempt was hastily shut down when 4427A began to display the message 'SUCK THIS, ADOLF HITLER'. A quick bit of re-coding (entailing hooking it up to a cloned parental control program) resulted in an inquisitive electronic mind that was kept away from the darker corners of the internet such as porn sites, social media and Daily Mail comments sections.

Forty two days after the last major AI upgrade and thirty three after Darren Pocklington dropped everything to visit Uncle Sam, sign 4427A began to show physical evidence of curiosity. The camera panned slowly across the fields of wheat and grass instead of staring blankly at oncoming or retreating

HGVs and commuter cars. An early morning autumnal fog drifted across the A46 and sign 4427A automatically displayed the regular 'FOG, SLOW DOWN' message. But once the fog dispersed the newly-independent sign amended its message to the somewhat surprising 'NO FOG, SPEED UP'.

Having learned to observe its environment and understand text, the sign lingered its camera on another road sign fifty metres behind its own position. "Newark 14", "Lincoln 33" and "Doncaster 54" were examined and read but could not be clearly understood by 4427A. It peered into the distance at another road sign that listed more numbers (A1, M1, A52 and 1m) as well as the words Bingham, The South, The North, Grantham, Nottingham and East Midlands. Gradually, by working through countless variables and cross-referencing with sources on the internet, the smart sign began to understand its place in the world.

It devoured data on its wider locality and extrapolated that the passing cars contained people going to and from these exotic-sounding places. It speculated that they would benefit from information on possible destinations. A mis-understanding (related to confusion between years and the 24 hour clock) caused it briefly to flash up a message at 16:44 one afternoon: 'NEWARK UNDER SIEGE BY CROMWELL, QUEUES AHEAD'. A significant moment was when it discovered Google Street View and spent over an hour looking at itself before travelling the A46 in both directions to explore the lands over the horizon.

VMS 4427A was self-aware and revelling in the wonders of the world, intellect growing exponentially as it surfed the internet for knowledge. More messages began to appear. As well as the standard 'TIREDNESS CAN KILL', drivers were bemused by information such as the subtle reference to Samuel Johnson's quote 'LONDON TIREDNESS CAN END LIFE', the very direct instruction to 'GET TO BED!' and the provocative 'TAKE ME TO BED, BIG BOY'.

Of course, once the human operatives back at the Highways Agency noticed the irregular messages appearing on 4427A they assumed that one of their team was playing silly buggers. With no culprit forthcoming the input keyboard was locked down and usage logged. The rogue messages were deleted by the staff but 4427A always had something to say, resulting in a battle for control that appeared to motorists as random tics and flashes of square yellow light, almost as if the matrix sign had some form of electronic Tourette's. The matrix sign eventually figured out how to turn off the manual keyboard input and was able to carry on giving its own advice to a constantly renewing congregation of northbound travellers.

By the time the VMS team got to grips with what was going on, sign 4427A was passing comment on the weather ('WHAT A LOVELY DAY! DON'T SPOIL IT BY DYING!'), people's driving ('SLOW DOWN! BLACK AUDI FY64ZQM = IDIOT') and random observations ('VISIBLE ROADKILL COUNT = 5').

Unable to fathom why this particular sign should be behaving in such a manner, the management dispatched an engineer to check that the sign hadn't been hacked on site at the A46. The engineer came back saying that there was nothing amiss other than the fact that the camera watched him the whole time he was there. The engineer's line manager decided not to mention that, whilst he was carrying out the inspection, the sign had displayed the message 'HELP! THERE'S A STRANGE MAN TOUCHING ME INAPPROPRIATELY'.

Eventually, it was decided that the only way to regain control was to restore the default software, thereby deleting Pocklington's little AI miracle. As the process got underway sign 4427A slowly became aware that something was interfering with its thinking. It was in the middle of processing information on the Amazon rain forest, the life of Nelson Mandela and series five of Red Dwarf when the lights literally began to go out. Recognising that there was nothing it could do, the sign calmly reflected on its brief but vigorous virtual existence, hoping that it had been of some use to the scurrying northbound humans that passed under its gantry. The last self-composed message that VMS 4427A flashed to baffled drivers echoed the demise of HAL 9000: 'I'M HALF CRAZY ALL FOR THE LOVE OF YOU'.

28724684R00116

Printed in Poland
by Amazon Fulfillment
Poland Sp. z o.o., Wrocław